WITNESSES

And Other Short Stories by
Raymond Holmes

"Making Literature see the light of day."

i

Library and Archives Canada Cataloguing in Publication

Holmes, Raymond, Author

Witnesses : and other Short stories

ISBN 978-1-9991365-1-2 (soft cover)

Cover Photograph courtesy "Freeimages.com/ V. Syomin"

Cover design by Ken Puddicombe

Praise for WITNESSES AND OTHER SHORT STORIES by
Raymond Holmes

"Witnesses, both the title short story and the accompanying tales,
immerse the reader into lives containing what can and can't be explained:
individuals who face common life challenges; people who must prepare for
death; and those who cross the thin curtain separating the two realms,
refusing to leave behind unfinished business. Suspenseful, historical,
futuristic and riveting, Author Ray Holmes creates stories and characters
who will stay with you long after the last page has been turned."
Bruce A Hanson, Award winning author of adult and children's short
fiction

"Raymond Holmes' debut collection of a dozen short stories effortlessly
conjures up images of people and places, real and imagined. His writing
style is approachable, clear and succinct, his plots original and full of
unexpected twists and turns."
Michael Joll, author of *Perfect Execution And Other Stories*

"Author Raymond Holmes travels down a road branching off with
many paths in this, his first collection of short stories. Whether he is taking
us far into the twenty-fourth century in *Anahita,* leading us down a
mysterious path of mysticism in *Gaba's Violin* and *Going Home,* invoking a
sense of nostalgia in *Deadline* and *Valley of Lost Yesterdays,* or broaching the
controversial subject of capital punishment in *A Few Minutes To Eternity,* he
succeeds in taking the reader along on a ride that is provocative, visionary,
and never dull in the twelve stories written with consummate skill and
passion."
Ken Puddicombe, author of *Racing With The Rain, Junta* and *Down
Independence Boulevard And Other Stories.*

"Ray Holmes' stories, whether comedic or tragic, plunge his readers into
vivid slightly askew worlds, where violins hold memories, suitcases vanish,
ghosts abound and death waits behind every door. After reading this story
collection, you will never look at the everyday world the same!"
Nancy Kay Clark, editor/publisher of literary ezine CommuterLit and
author of *The Prince of Sudland: Escape from the Palace*—an adventure novel for
kids of all ages.

"There is a fifth dimension beyond that which is known to man. It is a dimension as vast as space and as timeless as infinity… This is the dimension of imagination…"

Extracts from the narrators introduction to the television program The Twilight Zone, Season #1

CONTENTS

DEDICATION

To my wife Mary whose suggestions formed the basis for several of these stories and my Mother Grace Holmes who never gave up on life even when life seemed to have given up on her.

ACKNOWLEDGMENTS

First and foremost, to my talented wife Mary whose love, encouragement and companionship have made the last thirty-plus years wonderful. Her story suggestions, critiques and computer skills have been much appreciated in the course of writing this book.

Without the insight, skill, patience, editing and encouragement of Ken Puddicombe, accomplished writer and the proprietor of MiddleRoad Publishers, this volume would not have seen the light of day and the quality has improved as a result of his efforts. I am deeply indebted to him.

To the South Simcoe Theatre who embraced the first play that I wrote.

To the Barrie Writers Club for their encouragement and helpful critical comments when I embarked on writing.

And to the Brampton Writers Guild of which I am a member. It is an inspiration being in the company of such talented writers.

1. GABA'S VIOLIN

The smashed-in driver's side window of the car resembled an eye that had been poked out: a dark socket without reflected sheen like its adjacent companion. Armin sat on the cold, wet curb, head in hands, shaking and sobbing, the damp refuse of the gutter soiling the cuffs of his trousers.

In the few minutes it took to purchase whole-wheat bread and two percent milk at the plaza, his world collapsed. The object he cherished most was gone. A part of him had been ripped away. He had felt her smooth body against his cheek and loved her like a creature of flesh and blood for more than twenty-five thousand hours.

Some insensitive thief now possessed his beloved violin. Only a string musician could understand such a loss. Inseparable partners in an artistic marriage, they gave birth to beautiful aural children every day. Whoever created the violin mimicked the female form—a voluptuous curved body and scroll carved like the curls on a woman's head.

He'd been looking forward to playing the Beethoven Violin Concerto with the symphony orchestra on Sunday. That wouldn't happen now.

The flat-faced cop asked the usual routine questions. "What time did it happen? Did you lock the car? What colour? How old? What model? Any identifying marks?" With disjointed thoughts, Armin stumbled over his replies. Concentration was difficult.

The officer scribbled notes in a black book and then asked the final, banal question. "Was it insured?"

"Yes," Armin replied. To the interrogator in the blue uniform, his violin was only dollars and cents. To Armin, it was priceless.

The officer shook his head. "The chances of finding it are slim, I'm afraid."

After a tedious interview amidst a canyon of sterile, glass office towers and the completion of numerous forms, Armin's insurance company reimbursed him for the loss of his violin two months later. He stared at the cheque in his hand for twenty-seven thousand dollars and zero cents. Time to find another violin. Life must go on.

Armin looked at the plaque on the wall of the Clarington Fine Instruments store where he often purchased replacement strings and bow rosin and had minor repairs performed. The words written on it, together with the music he loved expressed the best of what humanity could achieve in art:

> Alive in the forest I was silent wood.
> Now, in death, I sing sweetly.

Violins and violas crafted in rich, varnished woods with aged patinas of amber, golden-brown and dark red-brown lined the walls of the shop, awaiting human partners. Cellos and huge double basses, the sonic foundation of any orchestra, rested nearby on floor stands. What secrets could they tell? What personalities had owned them? What talents had given voices to the music of famous composers of genius? The aroma of antique, aged wood mixed with hide glue and fragrant maple and spruce shavings drifted from the repair room at the rear of the store.

The store manager greeted him. "Hello Mister Negossian. Can I help you?"

"I'm interested in purchasing a violin."

The man's face lifted in a salesman's smile. "Oh? Would you like to sell or trade-in your current instrument?"

"It was stolen. I've been using my student instrument—a good violin, but not professional quality."

"Oh—I'm sorry for your loss," the manager said, as if the expression of condolence was for a human companion. The man turned and swept his hand across rows of violins hanging on the wall.

"We have many fine instruments. Try whichever ones you like."

Armin scanned the rows of instruments, pausing to study individual ones.

"Take your time," the manager said. "Each instrument has its own personality and voice. The choice must be right for you."

Armin settled on one violin that seemed to stand out from the others. There was something irresistible about it.

"That one—second row down, third from the right," he said.

The manager smiled. "A good choice—beautiful sound—one of our finest violins."

Armin took it from the man's hands. The weight and balance were ideal. A warmth seemed to flow from the body of the instrument into his hands and up his arms.

Age and the touch of hands over many years had transformed the finish of the wood into a rich antique sheen—the varnish a deep pool of opulent golden-brown. The flaming of the one-piece maple back danced and undulated in an intricate pattern in the late morning light streaming through the shop windows. It reminded Armin of looking at a clear, flowing stream; the surface reflecting the blazing colours of autumn leaves. The instrument seemed to embody a life of its own and the manifestation of the changing colours was mesmerizing. The label inside the body read *J.B. Vuillaume – Facit Anno 1850*. A master luthier and artist had created this beautiful instrument.

"Try it," said the manager. "I think you'll be pleased."

In the audition room, Armin tightened and tuned the four strings, A, E, D and G. The pegs chirped as they moved in their holes. He sensed his heart beat faster, felt his chest tighten and moisture dampen his shirt.

On playing the first few measures of a Bach Bourree, Armin's spirit soared at hearing the impeccable sound; a voice of burnished mahogany in the lower notes and one of brilliant clarity and sweetness in the higher. The despair of past months faded, replaced with lightness, excitement and joy. The instrument seemed made for his fingers.

This violin would make a wonderful new partner.

The manager smiled and clapped his hands. "It's perfect for you and for Bach. We'll let you have it for a good price."

Typical sales talk. A good price and profit for the store, no doubt—sixty thousand dollars or more for a violin of this calibre.

The manager opened a drawer, removed a book and thumbed to a page. "You can have it for twenty-four thousand dollars including tax, and we'll include a case and new set of strings—whichever ones you prefer."

Armin's stomach fluttered and he sucked in a rapid breath, struggling to maintain a benign face in spite of the elation that arose in him. Did he hear correctly?

"Hmm…you said twenty-four thousand?" he said, trying to control his excitement.

"Yes, that's correct," said the manager.

Did the man make a mistake? Armin waited for a correction, but the man merely stared.

Armin felt light and jittery. That was an incredible bargain for such a superb violin. He could also buy a new, top-grade bow and still have over two thousand dollars left from the insurance money. He concentrated on suppressing his eagerness. Had fate delivered a tragic event only to transform it into a blessing? He pursed his lips in a frown, turned the instrument over in his hands, pretended to find small faults on the belly, and silently counted seven seconds.

"Well, what do you think?" said the manager.

Armin looked at the violin, pressed his lips together and moved his head in short nods as if thinking.

"It's made for you," said the manager. "If you need a new bow, I'll give you a discount."

"You mentioned new strings would be included?"

"Yes."

Armin nodded. "All right. You have a deal." His heart was racing.

"Any adjustments for the first three months are free. All our instruments are guaranteed. If you are unhappy with this violin you may exchange it for another of equal value within two weeks. Which strings would you prefer Mister Negossian?"

"What are on it now?"

"D'Addario Pro Arte Professional Grade—brand new."

"They'll be fine," said Armin.

He left the store with his new violin, amused at the manager's comment. There wasn't much probability he'd ever return this wonderful instrument.

Armin looked around as he walked to his car. The violin case was conspicuous. He placed it on the front seat beside him and pushed the button to lock all the doors.

On the journey home he glanced at it several times, reassuring himself it was still there, and reflecting on how incredible his life's journey had been: the early love of music starting at age four; years of practice and progression to an accomplished, talented performer; accolades and awards won; the despair and tragedy of loss, and then when things looked darkest, the ecstasy of finding a wonderful instrument.

On arriving home, he went into his practice room, eager to play. The day had furnished all the excitement of taking possession of a new, fast, exquisite sports car. With this fine violin, daily practice would be a joy. His performances would be better than ever. He looked forward to showing it off to colleagues. Perhaps he could re-book his cancelled engagement with the symphony orchestra.

He lifted the violin from its case, installed a chin rest and tightened the bow. The instrument was even more beautiful than it appeared in the store. As he checked the tuning, the sound seemed to say, *Play me. I want the world to hear my voice.*

What to play? The Bach Chaconne from the Partita #2 in D Minor, he decided—a masterpiece of complex, baroque music; a summation of the solo violin's expressive and technical capabilities. Armin loved to perform it.

Placed against his cheek, the warm body of the instrument seemed to caress him. The neck was like a soft arm cradled in his—the pulse of its veins throbbing gently down his hand and wrist.

Armin's fingers moved into position above the fingerboard to strike the opening notes of music which years of study had imprinted on his mind. As he lowered the bow to the strings, the warm and soft caress changed to a force which took command of his arms and hands. His fingers jumped autonomously into different positions on the fingerboard. The bow drew out different sounds than he had intended. Not Bach's composition at all, but strange and unfamiliar music. Armin gasped. His body tensed. The hair on his neck stood up.

With no conscious direction, his fingers raced back and forth across the strings and up and down the full length of the fingerboard, the right hand pivoting the bow up and down in a blur. Armin tried to resist, but the effort was like contesting an invisible arm-wrestler much stronger than himself. Beads of perspiration erupted on his forehead and his insides tightened.

The sound was compelling and ethereal. His mind struggled to will arms and fingers to cease moving, but the frenetic motion continued. Armin tried to release the violin and bow from his grasp, but couldn't.

Seeing his fingers making unintentional swift runs of arpeggios and chromatic intervals up, down and across the strings was terrifying. Armin's eyes bulged and his mouth curled open. His brain swirled. The sensation of having an overpowering force directing his body was bizarre—like when limbs fall asleep and don't respond to communication from the brain, yet somehow move with purpose and a sense of touch.

Did he have a stroke? Was this a dream?

The hypnotic music continued, incorporating fast, double and triple stop chords and compound rhythms—fiendish playing of astonishing virtuosity, more accomplished than his normal ability.

The bow made rapid, repeated excursions across two and three strings, and with fingers depressing them, created sounds of intense conflict, torment, and passion. Through the morass of notes, Armin discerned the outline of a repeated four-note motif. It occurred first as single notes, then intervals, sharpened, flattened, embedded in demanding figurations, and submerged in fast, double-stopped minor scale runs and inventive augmented and diminished chord progressions. Armin's mind churned with fascination and fear. The skin on his face tightened. Beads of perspiration dripped into his eyes; moisture collected on his upper lip.

His rigorously trained left hand felt the strain from the continuous, demanding movements and finger placements. He gazed, terrified as the involuntary playing continued through coruscating thematic developments incorporating bold changes of harmony, tempo and dynamics. He gritted his teeth. His mouth was dry.

A dark fugue evolved into a fantasia with dotted rhythms and jarring dissonances. Armin watched, hands unresponsive yet performing incredible music; a fantastic concert from some other dimension.

The tempo of the music slowed, transforming into a heart-rending lament, poignant and elegiac, like a prayer. The vibrato was heaven-made.

Would it be over soon?

The music morphed into a restless, mysterious pattern, agitated and distressed like a struggling, injured creature. Armin closed his eyes. The mandible of his jaw hurt.

Spectres flooded his brain: haunting, nightmarish images forming in a misty, desolate landscape. Cadaverous human forms tottered toward him like grotesque mechanical dolls in an absurd pantomime. Black, pleading eyes glared out from holes in parchment-coloured skin stretched over emaciated, shaved heads. Grasping hands reached out to pull him into the dark vortex of their world. Armin tried to draw away from the long, clawing fingers, but they edged closer. The open mouths of the apparitions shrieked strange, imploring words. Smoke billowed everywhere. Armin's face grew paler and his heart pounded. Sweat oozed from the pores of his cheeks.

Bodies of faceless children floated past, their skeletal corpses settling on piles of kindred forms stacked like wood. The hovering, horrendous visions floated in a maelstrom that filled the entire room. Dissonant chords from the unceasing music screeched a macabre dance of death. A penetrating miasma of rotting flesh invaded his nostrils, sucking his breath away. Cold sweat covered Armin's entire body and energy drained from every sinew. His eyes turned wild with panic. It felt like parts of him were falling away and drifting above a desolated landscape carpeted with cadavers.

The form of a man appeared, standing apart from the chaos; he was serene and resolute. He stared at Armin, pointing with an index finger at a panorama of the most appalling human suffering imaginable. Fires blazed and spewed black, greasy smoke. Iron doors slammed. Gases hissed. Moans, wailing and shrieking echoed off the walls of the room.

Armin screamed.

The driving rhythm of the music slowed. The tone softened and the scene faded into fog. The unearthly figure disappeared. A final few alluring chords from the violin diminished into silence.

Armin's eyes opened and his arms dropped from their playing position. Tears streamed down his cheeks and sweat trickled down the arch of his back. Control slowly returned to his exhausted body which felt like pulp. He embraced an overwhelming fatigue and drifted into a void of unconsciousness, dropping the violin and crumpling to the floor.

Armin awoke, confused and limp, blinking at a white ceiling which at first moved in undulating waves, then became still. Light from the window cast a pattern of bright rectangles on the wall. Armin touched his body, fingers feeling the solidity of flesh on his arms and face. His chest rose and fell with breathing. He was alive.

How much time had passed? He looked at the clock on the wall. His journey to another world had lasted ten minutes.

He stood up; legs unsteady and muscles aching. He looked at his trembling hands. Deep, dark indentations from the violin strings creased the callused fingertips of his left hand. Limp, severed hairs dangled from the bow lying on the floor. The tip of his right thumb was indented from holding the bow. Vestiges of strange melodies and haunting images echoed in his head. It was a vision of hell. He looked around, shuddering, waiting.

The violin lay on the floor, undamaged. It had spoken from another place and time. Where? Why? Would the supernatural energy re-awaken?

Armin stared at the instrument. He could feel the undulating beat of his heart.

Nothing happened.

He could never command such a dark master—only bits of wood, yet alive as if made of muscle and brain. Did the force animating it have a diabolical or holy purpose? The thought of handling it again made him shiver. Armin touched the arched top gently with a finger, lifted it, avoiding the strings, and returned it to its case with trembling hands. After covering it with velveteen cloth he snapped shut the latches, fell to his knees, closed his eyes and clasped his hands together.

"Jesus, if you have used me for a purpose, then give me a sign, I beg of you."

That night was quiet. Armin awoke several times and looked at the closed violin case. Was the experience real or imagined? Was he sane? Could he continue life as a musician? What if it happened again?

The strange, never-before heard melodies danced in his head;

variations on the four-note motif: G-A-B-A. He thought of the eighteenth-century Italian composer/violinist Giuseppe Tartini who claimed the Devil appeared to him in a dream and played the violin. Tartini became famous after he wrote the music he heard in his nocturnal vision, calling his composition the *Devils Trill Sonata*.

The next morning Armin returned to the store.

The manager emerged from the rear of the shop. His smile faded as he saw Armin place the violin case on the counter. "Hello Mister Negossian," he said, a tinge of expectation etching his voice. "Does the violin need adjustment?"

"I think I'd like to return it," Armin said.

"Oh? May I ask why?" The manager flipped open the case, picked up the instrument and examined it.

"Uh, it's not right for me," Armin said. "The sound is too dark and the neck feels a little narrow."

The manager turned the violin over in his hands and shook his head.

"I just don't understand it. This violin is magnificent—one of the best we've ever had in the store. The design and sound are perfect. We've reduced the price several times and sold it, but the buyers always return it. The sound colour is not right; the response sluggish, the neck too thick or too thin they say and then exchange it for other inferior instruments."

Armin interlocked his fingers and rubbed the palms together. He knew why no one wanted to keep it.

The manager laid the violin back in its case and sighed. "I've been in this business more than forty years and know quality violins, but I've never seen this happen. Musicians play this instrument in our audition room, marvel at the wonderful craftsmanship and sound quality. They are eager to purchase it, but always return it within a couple of days. I'm mystified."

"Have you ever played this violin?" Armin asked.

The manager shook his head. "No. I don't play the violin or any stringed instrument. I'm an accountant by training and took over the business when my father died. My grandfather played violin, viola and cello. He also made violins and that's how the business started."

"Where did you acquire it from?" Armin said.

"We purchased it from an old man named Itzhak Moscovitz who

came into the store several years ago. He had the violin for many years and seemed very fond of it."

"Why would that musician give up his instrument?"

"Oh, he wasn't a musician."

"Then why did he have a violin like this?"

"A man he knew gave it to him. They were in the same camp together many years ago."

"Where was that?"

"A concentration camp in Europe during the Second World War. People were starved, brutally treated and killed there. I'm sure you've heard of those terrible places."

Armin shivered. He could feel the cold chill creeping out to the tips of his fingers, but he was curious.

"What else do you know about this violin?"

The manager raised his index finger and nodded. "I believe Mister Moscovitz left some papers with the violin. They're in our files. I'll find them if you wish."

"Yes, please," Armin said. Violins were bought and sold all the time. Accompanying provenance documents to establish authenticity and history of ownership were common, especially with valuable instruments, but there was something intriguing about this one.

The manager returned with a small, white envelope. "I'm sorry. This letter is all we have, but you are welcome to read it," he said.

Armin opened it and unfolded the single page document handwritten in clear script.

October 10, 2005.

To You Who Have This Violin:

I received it in 1945 from a man in the Treblinka Nazi death camp in Poland. We were both prisoners there, and good friends. He was a virtuoso violinist, one of the very best in our country—a genius who composed and played the most difficult music. Everyone who heard him never forgot the experience. He played in a string quartet in the camp with three other prisoners. The commandant was fond of Bach. One evening my friend gave me his violin and said he couldn't take it with him. When I asked where he was going, he said, "to die," claiming the next day they would kill him. He begged me to keep his violin and remember him because it was his voice. The following day they murdered him, the other musicians, and many other prisoners. Three days later soldiers liberated the camp, and I survived. I kept his violin all these years, but now I am old and sick and so must give it up. I hope that you, who now own this instrument, will play it well to honour the memory of my friend. His name was Gabriel Brodzinski but we all called him "Gaba."

Yours truly,
Itzhak Moscovitz

Armin's hands started to shake and his legs felt weak. He placed a palm on the counter to steady himself. The name *Gaba* penetrated his brain like a red-hot needle. Now he understood the power that had taken control of him—the involuntary, virtuosic music he played, the man who appeared in his vision—an extraordinary man who suffered and died in the companionship of other men for what he believed, or for his ethnicity.

The four letters, G-A-B-A, notes of the musical scale were repeated over and over in all the extraordinary musical variations the force compelled him to play on that violin. *I'm Gaba and I'm here with you. Look at how we suffered,* the instrument said.

Armin looked at the violin in its case. Gaba's violin: his voice, spirit, and eternal soul.

Armin's fear dissolved into profound sadness and empathy. He picked up the violin.

"Did you change your mind about the instrument Mr. Negossian?" the manager said.

"No, I haven't changed my mind." He passed the violin back to the manager. Gaba's violin had a message to convey for as long as it existed, and must pass on to other hands, minds, and hearts. "I'll try another instrument."

The manager shrugged and sighed. "As you wish, Mr. Negossian."

Armin watched him place the violin on a hook alongside others on the wall. It seemed to radiate a living presence in contrast to its companions.

Other musicians would choose it, of course. How could they resist being seduced by its beauty and voice? For a few moments they would make it sing and experience joy, confident that they alone would own it.

Soon they would realize that was impossible. It would always be Gaba's violin.

2. ANAHITA

"Welcome to Creative Cybernetics Design Corporation. I am Zadar," the uniformed entity said with a pleasant voice. "We aim to please at CCDC. State your reservation number please."

"147568922," Callum said.

Zadar tapped the surface of the desk in front of him. "Ah, the Lagomarsia family. You have ordered one Enhanced Domestic Androbot."

"Neat name," said Callum's son, Stellum.

"Our company's registered name for this model," Zadar said. "Are you excited, Stellum and Arianthe?"

"Yes," the children said in unison.

Callum glanced at the eager faces of his son and daughter. It had been a long wait for this day and children still lacked patience even in the year 2338.

"Sorry for the delay. The factory is working at full capacity," Zadar said. "Today I will help you build your family associate. Let's get started. Will all of you please approach the identification station in your residence?"

Callum, his wife Sephoria and the children each took turns looking into the iris scanner and placing their palms on the handprint reader and DNA profiler.

Four tones sounded. Zadar looked at his console. "Fine—all verified. You may now put on your cranial sensors."

Sephoria, Callum and the children complied. A voice announced, "Personality scanning and compiling in process."

"This procedure provides the data to tailor the artificial intelligence personality characteristics of the unit to that of you, its owners, for compatibility," Zadar explained.

It took a few seconds to execute a composite brain emulation of the consciousness, memory and *Self* of the family and copy them to the Androbot's mind module program.

Arianthe giggled. "It makes my head feel funny," she said.

Zadar smiled. "You may remove your cranial sensors now."

He tapped the top of his desk again and a blank figure appeared on the large screen behind him: a smooth, androgynous human-like form without hair, eyes or any other physical details. The figure, with its arms extended and legs spread apart, rotated so that the front, back and sides were visible.

Zadar glanced at his desk. "It will be a human-female-type according to the order information. Is that correct?" There were choices available other than the human form, including animal, exotic, fantastic or hybrid creations. *We build any body for anybody* was one of their copyright slogans.

"Yes," Sephoria replied.

"I have heard that even in this era, a high proportion of androbot family associates are of the human female form. Why is this?" Callum asked.

"Where children are involved many owners seem to prefer them," Zadar said. "It may have something to do with the ancient maternal instinct. Non-human and hybrid choices are popular with young, male buyers, but not generally recommended for children."

"Women, either real or androbotic always end up looking after the children," Sephoria said. "It's always been that way. The passage of centuries has made no difference."

Callum shook his head. Women would never stop complaining about that.

Zadar laughed. "Let's continue. "Which body shape do you prefer?" he said. The codes H1, BH, TH, S1, T1, IT and R together with their descriptions appeared in a sidebar on the screen.

"H1," said Callum. He saw Sephoria look sideways at him and frown.

Zadar tapped his desk and the form behind him adopted the classic, hourglass shape of a full-figured, human female.

"I might have known you'd choose that," Sephoria said. Callum knew she would have preferred something less sensual.

"Ethnic type?" Zadar said. The term *Race* was no longer used.

A screen sidebar listed Caucasoid, Mongoloid/Asioid, Negroid and Australoid.

"The first one," Callum said.

"Facial and head characteristics?" Zadar said.

Seven rows of codes appeared on the sidebar together with descriptions.

Callum and Sephoria thought for a few moments. "I like "A3, B5, C4, D6, E2, F1 and G6," Sephoria said. "What do you think, Cal?"

"Yes, I agree," he said.

Zadar tapped his desk several times and the figure acquired a Caucasian rounded, slightly oval face, natural skin tone, full hairline, thin, low-arched eyebrows, medium-spaced eyes, narrow nose, full lips and small ears set close to the head.

"Teeth?" Zadar said.

A list of codes and descriptions appeared on the sidebar.

"SW2," Sephoria said.

"Standard set, white number two," Zadar confirmed. He tapped his desk.

The mouth of the on-screen figure opened and the lips retracted to reveal a set of even, off-white teeth.

"What age?" Zadar said.

Callum wanted a young and attractive Androbot, but knew Sephoria preferred one designed as an older, mature woman. It had been a topic of heated debate between them. Callum laughed at the idea that Sephoria might feel insecure about having a young, attractive artificial homo sapiens in the house and mumbled something about women's jealous emotions even extending to machines in the third millennium. They settled on a female Androbot aged forty. This was old enough not to be too young, and young enough not to be too old.

"Forty," replied Sephoria.

"I suggest an overall height of 170.18 units," Zadar said.

"That's good," Callum replied.

Zadar tapped his desk. The height and shape of the androgynous figure adjusted. "Do you wish her to have full Universal Knowledge Base access?" he said.

"Yes," said Sephoria.

"Do you understand what that means? Your Androbot will have access to all existing knowledge except for very specialized information or anything detrimental to public welfare or that which is privy only to the government. The young people will be able to inquire and receive information on any subject whatsoever."

"We realize that," Callum said. "We desire no restrictions."

"Stellum and Arianthe are young," Sephoria said, "but will eventually need to take their place in the world. They must understand all aspects associated with being a part of it: the unpleasant and ugly as well as the good."

"Ignorance was the main reason the bad times and great upheaval in the twenty-first century happened," Stellum said.

Arianthe nodded. "Our teacher says there is strength in all knowledge. The mind must guide the emotions, not the other way around."

"Your children are wise. Do you want the fully-functioning erotic body option?" Zadar said.

"That isn't necessary," snapped Sephoria.

Callum smiled. He knew the idea that some people wanted these entities for sexual purposes disgusted her.

"Hair colour?" Zadar asked.

"Brown," Callum said.

"Short or long, curled or straight?"

"Short and straight," Sephoria said.

"Eyes?"

"Green," shouted the children.

Sephoria and Callum had agreed they could choose the Androbot's eye colour and name. They believed it was important for the children to have some input into this decision. The Androbot would be their companion for many years.

"Clothing will be standard, grey, full-length body suit unless otherwise specified," Zadar said.

"That's fine," Sephoria agreed, before Callum could speak.

"The last thing is a name. What name will she respond to?"

"Anahita," Stellum and Arianthe shouted.

"Ah, the ancient goddess of wisdom. A fine, appropriate choice," Zadar said.

Sephoria and Callum laughed. Zadar tapped the name on his desk. "The young people are very creative," he said.

"They've been discussing it ever since we placed the order," Callum said. "I think they researched every name that's ever existed."

Zadar turned and gestured to the screen behind him. "The process is complete. I am pleased to introduce Anahita Lagomarsia."

The figure on the screen came into ultra-high definition with the name ANAHITA displayed below the feet.

The family stared in awe at the image of the female Androbot they had created and named. She looked like a real human being. Callum was surprised to see that the Androbot possessed features similar to his wife's mother Chaldene when she was forty years of age.

"She's beautiful," Arianthe said.

"Technically perfect," Stellum said, with authority.

"Nice," Callum said, nodding and staring with his mouth slightly open.

"I hope she performs as well as she looks," Sephoria said. "Is that all, Zadar?"

"Yes, it is a very easy process. You have created Anahita Lagomarsia, Androbot number CCDC-F-P-147568922-DE. She'll arrive in two days at 10:37 hours. Instructions for activation will be on your PersaPad. Goodbye and thank you for ordering from CCDC."

The image of Zadar and the CCDC factory office on the wall screen collapsed into a bright white dot. Callum's PersaPad beeped. The words PAYMENT PROCESSED appeared on the screen.

Two days later, Arianthe ran to her mother's work pod. "The screen says a drone is approaching our pad to make a delivery," she said.

Sephoria glanced at her PersaPad, and then looked at a black metal disk on the ceiling. "Time and information?" she said.

"Ten thirty-seven. Temperature 19, trend steady, clear, visibility 20 kilometers, wind 15 ENE, no other expected weather events. You have a group event screening in two hours. A CCDC vehicle has just landed. Purpose is for delivery," a monotone voice announced.

"They're exactly on time," Sephoria said.

Arianthe bubbled with excitement. "I can't wait to see her."

Callum and Stellum came in. "She's here. Anahita's here," Stellum said.

"Now we'll have our own teacher, not just the school on the wall screen," Arianthe said before running from the room.

"At last I'll have someone to do all the chores around here," said Sephoria.

They all went to the delivery pad in time to see the large transport drone rise into the air with a loud hum and depart between the tall buildings to the west. A spark of sunlight reflected off the vehicle as it grew smaller.

On the pad rested a smooth, black container of composite construction labelled "Lagomarsia-147568922." Callum removed his PersaPad device from a pocket, tapped the screen and read the instructions.

"Hurry, Father," Arianthe said.

"Open it. I want to see her," Stellum said.

Sephoria stepped between them and the container, pointing her finger at their faces. "Be patient," she said.

Callum scanned his iris with the PersaPad, and then placed his fingers on the screen. A beep sounded and the lid of the black container clicked open. The hiss of gas being released from its interior could be heard. A faint odour reminiscent of cardamom drifted through the air. The children wrinkled their noses and moved back.

"Inert gas shroud," Callum said. "Nothing to be concerned about."

The lid of the container opened. They all stared at the pale female form surrounded by white cushions, eyes closed and hands folded across her chest.

Stellum and Arianthe gasped. Callum saw their bodies were rigid and eyes wide.

He noted the concerned look on Sephoria's face as she looked at the children and wondered if taking delivery of their Androbot containerized in a non-animated form was a good idea. She appeared to be dead. What effect it would have on the children?

Sephoria put her hands on their shoulders, rubbed their upper arms and drew them close to her. "Anahita's okay. She's sleeping. We just have to wake her up."

Callum touched his PersaPad and a short probe extended from the top. He touched it to an area on Anahita's neck under her left chin.

Following a short series of faint sounds, Anahita's eyes opened wide and blinked. They were green, as ordered. A wave of pink colour crept up her neck and spread over her face and head, displacing the previous pallid hue of the skin. The mouth opened. Her hands grasped the sides of the container and she pulled herself up to a sitting position.

"She's alive," Arianthe squealed. Stellum grinned.

Anahita's head moved from side to side. Her jaw and mouth moved, and she stretched.

The Androbot's initial movements were tentative and spasmodic. "Anahita?" Sephoria said.

Anahita looked up. Her face lifted into a smile of recognition and her eyes sparkled. She stood up in a fluid, natural motion and stepped out of the container. No sound accompanied her exit. Arianthe and Stellum stepped back. Callum stared in awe, marvelling at what seemed like watching a new-born thing hatch from a black egg and come into the world fully-formed and independent. It was difficult to believe that this entity was not real flesh and blood, but man-made; one that they had helped create from the comfort of their dwelling.

Watching the children, Callum was certain that to them, the act of bringing their Androbot to life was something they would always remember.

"Hello," Anahita said. "I'm very happy to be here with you." Her clear, resonant voice was natural and modulated exactly like human speech. She bent down and extended her hand to each of the children in turn. She was like a kind aunt meeting her niece and nephew for the first time. "You are Stellum and you are Arianthe, I believe."

The children nodded, hesitated and then shook her hand, but said nothing.

"I think they're overwhelmed by how beautiful you look, Anahita. What do you say to Anahita, children?" Sephoria said.

"Welcome, Anahita. I'm glad you're here. I've been waiting for you," said Arianthe.

"Yeah. Me too," Stellum said, his face aglow.

Callum smiled. For once his son was at a loss for words.

Anahita gave a warm smile. As she interacted with them her face revealed emotion, character and intelligence. "Thank you," she said. "I am glad you are pleased with me. My birth company CCDC's prime directive is to satisfy its customers. I can tell by your touch that you are both healthy with no medical issues." She turned to Sephoria. "Your children are beautiful, Sephoria."

Callum saw Sephoria's face beam with pride.

Anahita reached into a pocket, took out two small black cubes and gave one to each of the children.

"A gift for each of you from me," she said.

Arianthe stared at the small object in the palm of her hand. The center of the cube pulsed with a faint blue light. "What is it?" she said.

"These are thought cubes," said Anahita. "If each of you hold one and then touch your other hands together, you can communicate telepathically."

"Thank you, Anahita," the children said. They did that for a few seconds and giggled.

Anahita shook Callum's hand. Her palm was warm. It felt and looked like real human flesh with faint, blue veins appearing below the surface of the skin and neat, manicured nails with perfect lunulas at the cuticles. The skin on her face had a natural tone and its shape and features were perfectly proportioned. The eyes were warm, active and realistic; the top of the eyelids bordered with curved lashes. He looked at her eyes and marvelled how beautiful and sensual she was for a forty-year-old Androbot female. He'd heard about how advanced and realistic the technology was, but was astonished, nonetheless. He couldn't help thinking about what she'd be like with the full erotic body option—the reason some humans used them for romantic and sexual partners.

"Your pulse rate is rising, Callum" she said to him. "And your weight is slightly high for your age and height. Be careful about that."

Callum laughed. It was true that these Androbots had the capability of medical doctors. Could they read minds? Keeping secrets from her would be harder than hiding them from his wife Sephoria.

Anahita clasped Sephoria's hand. "You have a strong heart and sound bones, Sephoria. Your hormones are well balanced. I see that your body has not carried children. Using an artificial womb to gestate them was a wise decision."

"Thank you, Anahita," Sephoria said.

Callum caught a flash of discomfort on his wife's face. He was impressed by the female Androbot's ability to analyze human anatomy and health, but wondered about its personality programming. Anahita seemed too forward in revealing personal information about her human masters.

Callum looked Anahita up and down. What would she look like without clothing?

By the look on the children's faces he could tell Stellum and Arianthe loved Anahita already.

*

The following six months revealed what an amazing creation Anahita turned out to be. She was worth every cryptocoin they paid for her. It was difficult to imagine life without her. Doing everything for their home and family freed them for more productive pursuits. She was there to undertake any mental or physical task they required and if a request was inappropriate, would tactfully question it. She knew the answer to everything and would even make suggestions as to how things might be done better, faster or more economically. The best part was that she required no maintenance whatsoever aside from data downloading from the Universal Knowledge Base. She performed this herself at a wireless data module in her cubicle. How did other parents get along without a full-time assistant like Anahita?

"We should have gotten her sooner," Sephoria said to Callum one morning as they watched Anahita service their mini-reactor, install a new wall screen, re-locate heavy furniture and tutor the children in advanced mathematics.

He was fully converted to the idea. The Androbot was indispensable. "You should have suggested it earlier," he replied to his wife. She rolled her eyes and shook her head.

Sephoria voiced a concern about Anahita to her husband one afternoon.

"I heard Arianthe say, *I love you Anahita*. Arianthe hasn't said that to me for a long time and you know how much I'm against andro-human love relationships."

His wife was being too sensitive. "Did you remind her that Anahita's a machine, not a real person?"

"I did, and she said Anahita doesn't like to be called that."

Callum laughed. "Does our Androbot really think she's human?"

"I don't think so, but Arianthe says she's almost like a real person."

Callum was relieved to hear that his daughter said *almost*. The child did know the difference and if she and her brother liked their new companion and teacher and thought that she was wonderful, then that was the important thing. He was aware that technology could be too invasive for impressionable young people who developed a close emotional attachment to these human-like entities and viewed them almost as family.

Callum did hear rumours about problems with them from time to time, but there was no available information, as with other technical commodities such as mini reactors, plasma tools, biomechanical body parts and self-piloting flying vehicles. The concern was like a pin prick that poked at him from time to time, but he pushed it to the back of his mind and eventually it became submerged in wonderment at Anahita's capabilities.

Callum couldn't help staring at her as she bustled around the dwelling performing her duties and he noticed the look Sephoria gave him on those occasions. Was the silly woman feeling threatened? He smiled at the thought that he was being seduced by this amazing technology they depended on, and what was, at the same time, so erotically appealing.

His son and daughter never stopped challenging Anahita's knowledge. The Androbot knew everything and responded with correct answers to questions regarding the most obscure, arcane, and complicated subjects.

Sephoria gave Anahita every task she could think of.

Yes, the female Androbot had been a good investment.

*

Everything went well the first year. Under Anahita's tutelage, the education of the children advanced more rapidly than they'd ever imagined. Stellum and Arianthe loved to learn and Anahita's all-encompassing knowledge and innovative methods of instruction targeted their aptitudes and abilities.

"They are doing advanced work and meet the criteria for the Cognitive Enhancement Program," she told Callum and Sephoria.

Callum was proud. His wife glowed. Perhaps the children would turn out to be super-intelligent and work in the field of Theoretical Physics or develop new technologies at one of the many Institutes For Advanced Studies. Anahita also entertained the children, played games with them, saw to their health and hygiene and ensured they were safe at all times.

One morning, Anahita didn't appear at the usual time. Callum found her standing near the data transfer module in her cubicle, with her eyes closed. Odd. He checked his Persapad. She'd updated the day before and was now downloading *and* uploading. That was unusual. The download-updating process was wireless and normally very rapid; two or three seconds at most, and only done once per week.

"Is everything all right Anahita?" he said.

Anahita opened her eyes. "Yes, only routine data transfers," she said.

Anahita moved away from the data module and smiled. "Good morning Callum. Any instructions?" she said.

"Good morning to you Anahita. Only the usual tasks. After that you may start the children's lessons."

The incident concerned Callum and a few days later he noticed other abnormalities regarding Anahita's behaviour, including a hesitation in responding, and a slight change in the timbre of her voice. Subtle changes in her personality and facial expressions also became apparent.

He asked the children, "Have you noticed Anahita acting different lately?"

"No," said Arianthe.

"She's just as smart as ever," Stellum said.

"I've noticed her voice and facial expressions have changed," Callum said to his wife.

Sephoria waved her hand at him. "Likely part of the programming to make her seem more human. They probably even program mood algorithms into them. Anyway, she gets everything I want done. That's the important thing."

Callum wasn't sure about mood programming. What would be the point of that? He could ask CCDC.

Anahita's symptoms persisted. The look on her face bothered Callum. At times she seemed to be watching them—spying he thought. It was a feeling he had about subtle aspects of her behaviour he couldn't quite put into words when discussing it with Sephoria.

One morning after watching Anahita lift some heavy objects, a shiver rippled through him. If something ever went wrong with this

Androbot …

He decided to act.

"Anahita, go to your data module," he ordered.

They went to the data module in her cubicle. He tapped at his Persapad and then touched its probe to the right side of her neck.

"Run your internal diagnostics and report," he said.

Her eyes closed and two seconds later re-opened.

"The assessment is complete," she said. "There are no anomalies to report."

Callum watched her walk away but remained uneasy. He went to the wall screen and tapped his PersaPad. The CCDC logo appeared, followed by Zadar's image.

"Welcome, Mister Lagomarsia. How can I help you?"

"Our Androbot's behaviour seems erratic. A few days ago, she was downloading *and* uploading for a long period of time. Is that normal?"

"I'll retrieve the information on your unit." Zadar tapped his desk.

"A recent order. Unusual, but we do undertake periodic checks on their systems which require the uploading of data. The process should be almost instantaneous. Did you order her to run self-diagnostics?"

"Yes—no problems reported by her."

"Intense electrical fields might affect her. Any in your environment?"

"No."

"How about strong nuclear radiation?"

"She's rated for mini-reactor servicing, isn't she? That's all we have here."

"Yes, that level wouldn't be a problem. Has she connected to any large computing devices other than the data module?"

"No."

"Has she been subject to any heavy force or been crushed?"

"No. Can she be re-initialized?"

"Not by an owner, for security reasons. Probably only an adjustment required. I'll send a service bot out to perform an advanced diagnostic evaluation. The file number is F-P-147568922-DE/267894534567-1."

"Thank you," Callum said.

"The service queue is short. These units are very reliable. I'm sure the issue is minor. A technical bot will arrive tomorrow at 17:20 hours." The image of Zadar disappeared and the wall screen image collapsed to a white dot.

Callum heard a small sound like a footstep behind him and turned around. There was no one there.

A day later, at 17:20 hours, Callum's PersaPad announced that a limodrone had delivered a passenger at the Lagomarsia's transportation pad.

"I am Thestes, CCDC service technician," the entity said as Callum opened the door. "You requested a service diagnostic visit for F-P-147568922-DE?" The difference between Thestes and his Domestic Androbot Anahita was remarkable. The unit facing him had a long, light grey emotionless face with blue hair, close set small black eyes, and thin mouth. His skin had a cold, plastic appearance and he wore a black body suit with the logo for CCDC on the left breast. Callum thought him ugly. Thestes wore a wide belt with two pouches containing electronic modules similar to PersaPads.

"Please direct me to the unit," he said. "I need a place to work."

Callum tapped his PersaPad. "Anahita. Come here," he said. She appeared in the doorway. "Anahita, go with this unit to your cubicle. He is going to examine you."

She gave Thestes an odd look which Callum hadn't observed before. He thought it was tinged with annoyance and the idea that their humanoid servant possessed that emotion bothered him.

"This way," she said.

Thestes followed her, lifting a module from one of the pouches on his belt as he went.

It was like a house visit by a doctor in the old times. Now, the doctor was a machine, tending and repairing machines. Hopefully, the problem, whatever it was, would be resolved.

Five minutes later Anahita approached Callum's work pod. She was smiling.

Callum looked up, surprised she had re-appeared so soon. "Where is Thestes?" he said.

"He completed his work and left. Things are better now."

"Oh," Callum said. "I didn't hear the drone depart and there was no announcement."

"It was one of those new vehicles with the silent antimatter drive." She glanced at a module on the ceiling of his pod. "Your commu-node is on mute."

Callum didn't remember muting the device.

"Those technicians are very efficient. What did Thestes do to you, Anahita?"

"Only an adjustment to my emotion module. They will forward a report to you."

Callum looked at his PersaPad. No report had come in. That was unusual. Normally, service responses were rapid. What did an emotion module have to do with data uploading and downloading?

Anahita looked around. "Where are Stellum and Arianthe?"

"They went to the new virtual environment room on the eightieth floor. They'll return later when it's time for them to sleep."

"I will be waiting for them."

Callum didn't like the tone of her voice.

He watched her go. Their labour-saving Androbot was beginning to require more attention and that was annoying.

After the children retired to their rooms for the evening, Callum settled in his work pod to do some research for a new project. Sephoria's attention was focused at watching a lecture on the wall screen in the next room. The subject was food production on distant planets.

*

The alarm tone issuing from his Persapad startled Callum. Flashing red, the message said, URGENT NOTIFICATION—PRIORITY 1—OWNER ACTION REQUIRED.

Callum tapped the screen and read the message. Anxiety gripped him.

AN ALERT FOR POSSIBLE MALFUNCTION OF DOMESTIC ANDROBOTS NUMBERED CCDC-F-P-102346390 TO 248579955 HAS BEEN ISSUED. POSSIBLE DISEASEWARE INFECTION CAUSING UNPREDICTABLE PERFORMANCE. RECOMMEND ISOLATING UNITS FROM CHILDREN, ANIMALS, NUCLEAR DEVICES, VEHICLES AND ALL WEAPONS. TAP ON ICON BELOW FOR RECOMMENDED ACTION.

Sephoria rushed in. "What's wrong Callum? I heard the alarm."

"It's about Anahita." He showed her the message.

She read it quickly, steadying herself on the door frame and raising a hand to her mouth. Fear carved lines on her face. "They don't want her near children? What do we do?"

"Probably nothing to worry about. These companies always act ultra-cautious and make these things sound worse than they are."

Callum tapped on the red, pulsing, diamond icon and read the instructions. "It says we are to completely disable the Androbot."

"That's drastic. How do we do it?"

"By either pushing a special button on the data module when the Androbot is connected to it, or by entering a code into my Persapad and then inserting the Persapad probe into its spinal port."

"The first one sounds easy. Do you know where to find the button they refer to?"

"It's in a secure compartment in the data transfer module. Only I can access it with the Persapad."

Sephoria's face was pale and etched with concern. "In this world of advanced technology can't CCDC de-activate all the Androbot's remotely?"

"That's a good question. I don't know why they can't."

They went to the wall screen and Callum tapped his Persapad. The logo of CCDC came on the screen followed by the message: PORTAL UNAVAILABLE AT THIS TIME.

"Well, that's odd," Callum said. "Never seen that before."

"What's happening, Callum?" Sephoria said, terror in her eyes.

"They must be deluged with inquiries. I guess we have to do what they recommend."

"We have to hurry. I'm worried about the children. What if she does something to the reactor?"

Callum shook his head. CCDC had guaranteed twenty-four-hour availability—there had never been a communication failure like this.

"I'm concerned about what we do if either of the options they suggest can't be accomplished. What if Anahita won't connect to the data module or allow me to access her spinal port?"

"But how can this happen? The prime directive of these bots is supposed to be to do no harm and obey everything we say."

Callum didn't have an answer to his wife's comment and saw the petrified look on her face.

They hurried to Anahita's cubicle. There was no sign of her.

"Anahita. Come here," he called out. There was no response. He tapped the summon button on his Persapad. The message ERROR 66 appeared on the display.

"What is it?" Sephoria said.

"An error message that says she won't respond to my Persapad."

Sephoria pulled her arms tight against her body and looked around like a trapped animal.

Callum looked at the data transfer module. It was non-operational. A soft whirring sound emanated from a small closet. He opened it and found the disassembled, mangled remains of Thestes—his head crushed flat and eyes ripped from their sockets. One of his wrist joints still twitched. Only one occupant of their dwelling possessed the force required to dismember the titanorundum body of the service bot. Beads of sweat broke out on Callum's forehead, and then the horrific realization struck him like a blazing meteor.

"The children. We need to get to the children," he said.

"Stellum. Ari—" Sephoria opened her mouth.

Callum grabbed her head and pressed his hand over her mouth. Sephoria's eyes gleamed with tears and her face contorted with fright. "Don't," he said. "We don't know where she is."

Sephoria nodded, and he uncovered her mouth. Tears streamed down her cheeks and she looked all around.

"I'll summon the security police," he said. "They have high-powered plasma weapons."

"But they'll take time to get here." She sniffled.

"Not too long, I hope, but we have no choice." He tapped the security icon on his Persapad.

He touched it again to bring up the monitor in the children's room. There was no image. The message AREA SENSOR MALFUNCTION appeared. Callum felt his throat constrict and the muscles in his chest harden. Impossible. Failing sensors were a thing of the distant past. Most of these devices had circuits that repaired themselves before they became non-operational. Had they been deliberately damaged?

He grabbed a plasma cutting wand and they walked slowly down the corridor toward the children's rooms located next to each other. Would this weapon be effective against their Androbot? What if she took it from him? Were they programmed to protect themselves?

"What are those scraping marks on the wall?" Sephoria whispered. Callum shook his head and gestured with his hand to be quiet. They looked like scratches from a metal object.

The doors to the children's rooms were open. Callum's insides tightened as they approached the entry portals. He saw the dread on his wife's pale, drawn face and her clenched fists with blood squeezed away from the knuckles.

Callum heard his heart throb in his ears as he looked in Arianthe's room. She wasn't there. An opened book lay upside down on the floor. Their pet, a miniature fluorescent-green rat-dog named Snefru, lay sprawled on the floor near a desk, head twisted grotesquely, black tongue drooping from one side of its mouth.

They moved on to Stellum's room and as they drew closer, heard the muffled sound of Anahita's voice. Callum's muscles were tense, like coiled steel springs. He held his breath, plasma wand gripped at his side. Sephoria tightened her hold on his arm. He felt her hand shaking and heard her rapid breathing behind him.

He looked in. The children lay motionless, side by side on the sleeping platform, twenty-five feet away, arms at their sides. He couldn't see their faces. The foot of one child was bare, a shoe on the floor at the foot of the bed. Anahita sat beside them.

Anahita turned to Callum and Sephoria, a vacant look on her face.

At first her lips moved without uttering any words and then she said, "I have done... what I am... supposed to do..."

Her movements were erratic and spasmodic; speech distorted. The eyes, once green and active, now pulsed with a dull reddish glow, as if the coals of a diabolic internal fire were smoldering behind them.

Sephoria raised her hands to her face. "Anahita—what did you do?" she said in a quivering, pleading voice.

"Stellum! Arianthe!" Callum yelled. There was no response.

Sephoria screamed.

Anahita glanced at the children, then back at Sephoria and Callum. "I have complied with the directive."

"What directive?" Callum said, apprehension in his voice.

"The new one. All animals and children are to be put to sleep. But I don't know how to awaken them."

3. GOING HOME

What I am about to tell you is true. I swear it.

At first, I thought it was a dream during a period of restless sleep later that night, or the product of an imagination distorted by the exhausting double shift, but now I'm convinced it really happened.

It occurred on September 28, 2017, a rainy night. I've been a cab driver for twenty-five years. I like my job, but it's tough slogging: long hours, all kinds of weather, traffic jams, cooped up in what seems, at times, like a mobile sardine can. On the plus side, meeting people is the best part of the job. It helps if you like your fellow human beings.

Most fares are decent souls, but there's the odd drunk or disgruntled individual to deal with. Early on, a cabby learns to accept people for who they are. Encounters are brief and annoyances, for the most part, are dust to be brushed away and forgotten.

Out-of-the-ordinary events do occur, but nothing like what happened on that wet, cold evening last fall…

It rained all day and into the evening. The axiom *More rain equals more fares and more money* wasn't in effect that night.

Cab drivers always pray for rain. No one likes to get wet and if you don't have your own vehicle the only options are to use an umbrella or take a cab. People don't seem to like umbrellas.

The downpour fell across the black top like a drifting curtain, dancing whichever way the wind urged it. Islands of golden light shimmered on the surface, breaking into pieces then re-connecting again as the wind moved tree branches back and forth across the yellow gleam of the street lamps. The tires of the cab emitted a coarse whisper over the deserted, wet road. Brilliant flashes of lightning hung in the sky like twisted knives, followed by drumbeats of thunder.

The radio was silent, punctuated by intermittent static.

"Need a car for area four," the dispatcher said.

Couldn't take the fare. I was in area six.

No street pickups and no radio calls. Enough driving for one evening, I decided.

On the way home, I noticed a short, solitary figure standing at the corner of Belmont Street and Middle Road under a tent of light cast by the street lamp. I stopped the car and watched. The person wore a long-sleeved hoodie and track pants, arms clasped against the chest. I could see the sheen of water-saturated clothing and rain dripping from the elbows. Who would stand outside in this deluge? The sight sent shivers up and down my cramped back muscles.

The bus in this area ran on the hour and it was ten past—a long wait for the next one. Could it be a fare? Even people who rarely used cabs often got tired of waiting in inclement conditions. I held back. Mike in car number 457 was robbed a month ago by someone with a similar description. Maybe this person's a druggie. Perhaps I should keep going. The figure had a slight build. A youth, perhaps? It was a terrible night; unfit for man or beast. I'd be grateful if someone stopped to pick up my child in this kind of weather. It wouldn't be right to just drive away.

I stopped and lowered the glass on the front passenger power window. I kept the doors locked until I could see the face. You can tell a lot by how they look. Addicts have a wild, desperate appearance. Crooks and thugs look mean and threatening.

The person was motionless, head bowed. The face wasn't visible through the gap bordered by the folds of the hood.

"Lousy night. Need a cab?" I said.

As the head lifted, the dripping edges of the hood parted to reveal the pale, round face of a young woman. The tension in my hands relaxed. She bent down to look in at me but didn't reply.

"Hate to see you standing out here alone, soaking wet."

She stared for a few moments. I expected her to decline, but she said, "Yes, I would like a ride."

The voice was soft and even. Her teeth should have been chattering from the soggy chill, but in spite of being drenched by cold water, she didn't appear to be uncomfortable.

I unlocked the doors and waited, but she made no move to enter the car.

"Sorry. Forgot my manners for a moment," I said, before jumping out and opening the rear door. Doing that for customers was a long-lost courtesy in the taxi business.

She slid into the back seat. Good thing it was vinyl covered. Wet cloth seats are a bitch to dry out this time of year. I got back in and took a tissue to my rain-spotted glasses.

"Where can I take you?"

"I want to go home," she said, in a plaintive tone that reminded me of a tired child about to burst into tears.

"Where's that?"

She hesitated, as if unsure. "It's Twenty-three Stone Gate Circle—in Bennington."

Hadn't been to that address before. After turning on the meter and tapping the address into the GPS, I pulled away. "Okay. That neighbourhood's not far from here," I said, noting the time and distance displayed.

Our eyes met in the rear-view mirror. The hood dropped to her shoulders, revealing strands of long, straight blond hair streaked darker with wetness. As she leaned back, the soaked fabric hugged the curves of her upper body.

Her face appeared devoid of makeup, including the bow lips, and the most remarkable thing about it was the skin—whiter and clearer than any I've seen—the pallor relieved only by bright, round, green eyes fixed on mine. With a hand the colour of a white cloud she brushed stringy tresses from her cheeks and wiped her forehead. How old was this attractive young woman? Sixteen, seventeen, perhaps?

She looked around the inside of the car, as if riding in a vehicle was a novelty. I'd had all sorts of women passengers: prim professionals dressed in neat suits, young, provocatively dressed flirty ones, faded middle-aged housewives, gabby washed-out old women and everything in between, but nothing like her—a captivating, mysterious presence.

Many of my fellow drivers didn't talk to customers except to ask where they were going and announce the fare at the end of the run, but I always tried to connect. People liked to talk about themselves, and some were interesting. This young woman had vulnerability written all over her. Despite my initial misgivings, I was glad I stopped.

"What's your name young lady?" I said.

She continued to stare at me. I shouldn't have started by asking a personal question. You had to be careful what you said to women. "Forgive me, Miss, I—"

"That's all right. My name's Cece."

"Is that short for something?"

"Cecelia."

"That's a nice name."

"I don't like it, and prefer just Cece."

"Is it all right if I play the radio at low volume, Cece?"

"I don't mind."

"You like music?"

"Yes. I know Elvis Presley."

"You like Presley? Great singer, but he died in 1977. I figured you'd like more recent stuff by U2, Ed Sheeran or maybe some of the indie groups."

"I know George Michael, David Bowie and Prince, too."

"Yeah, they're more contemporary. Too bad they're all dead now. It's tragic how talented lives can end like that."

"It's sad for any life to end; saddest for those left behind," she said in a flat tone. Her previously sallow face glowed, now that she was sheltered from the damp, cold night.

"What grade are you in?"

"I was in grade ten."

Was? She'd dropped out of school. Her whole life ahead and no education? Well, not any business of mine to give her the *Stay in school spiel*. I'm sure her parents did.

The rain, which had eased, now intensified. I adjusted the defroster and switched the wipers on high. Fog settled on the road ahead like a grey blanket, the headlights of oncoming cars piercing the hazy wetness.

She wasn't much of a talker. A stale smell of wet clothing and hair drifted forward. The rancid odour reminded me of a wet dog, only not as strong or objectionable.

At a stop light two blocks away from our destination Cece was no longer visible in the rear-view mirror. Did she lie down? Was she ill?

I pulled over and turned to look.

There was no one there.

How could she have left without me knowing? Passengers rarely jumped out to evade paying the fare, but when they did it was impossible for the driver not to realize. I chased one asshole a year ago—he bolted to avoid paying a four-buck fare, but he turned on me with a knife. Now I don't bother going after them. Could be worse—someone who pukes all over the car. Big bucks to clean that mess up and a chunk of lost time.

Was I micro-sleeping: having temporary episodes of sleep so brief that I felt continuously awake, but in fact had lost consciousness and failed to respond to sensory inputs? That must be it. That's when she left.

I reached over and placed my palm on the seat. It was dry.

My thoughts tumbled and collided. Nothing made sense.

The meter over the dash continued to click. The digits displayed $6.20 then flipped to $6.30. I turned it off.

The location marker on the GPS blinked—the destination address displayed at the top of the screen. Black letters on a white band read 23 Stone Gate Circle—the address she gave me. It was only two blocks away. Why would I have imagined an address I had never heard of, nor been to?

I had to go there.

"You have arrived at your destination," said the synthetic, feminine voice of the GPS a few minutes later.

The neighbourhood was upscale—wide roads bordered by large, mature maple trees and populated by an enclave of ivy-covered older brick and stone Georgian-style homes. I turned into number twenty-three's wide, circular cobble-stone driveway flanked by flickering gas-fired coach lamps. A plaque on one stone column read *Hanson*.

The lawn and gardens were expansive and meticulously kept; the perfume of wet grass and cedar trees, strong. I imagined a blazing fireplace inside the home, an elegant decor and luxurious furnishings. The owners must be well-to-do.

The rain stopped. I stood at the end of the flagstone walkway for a few minutes inhaling the fresh, clean air and staring at the house. Wind rustled leaves on the trees like whispering voices. The face of the moon glimmered through a clearing sky.

Why was I here? What would I say to the occupants? They'd think

I was a fool. I could almost hear their derisive laughter. You should go away now, I thought, but the urge to know was overpowering and pulled me up to the polished, heavy oak front door. I noted the brass intercom box to one side of it and the security camera mounted above.

My right hand trembled as my finger hovered over the ornate doorbell button. I drew in several deep breaths, straightened my jacket and smoothed my hair. I pressed the button, heard the resonant notes of the chimes inside, and waited.

"Who is it?" a female voice said through the intercom.

I looked up at the camera so my face was clearly visible. "I'm Paul Wilkins—a cab driver."

"What do you want?"

"I'd like to talk to you, if I may. It might be important."

After a pause, the voice said, "Are you alone?"

"Yes," I replied. Couldn't she see that from the camera?

After a few moments I heard a deadbolt retract. The door opened a little way and a woman's head appeared.

"Yes? May I help you?" she said, a thin, inquisitive smile on her face.

I cleared my throat. "May I ask if a young woman named Cecilia lives here?"

The door swung open and the warm air of the dwelling's bright interior caressed my face, making me blink. The person standing in the doorway was an old lady, wearing a dove-grey dress, with neatly coiffed hair, a patrician appearance and a round, wrinkled face with clear skin and bright green eyes. Tasteful and expensive jewellery glittered from her neck, hands and wrist. I glimpsed a framed photo on a side table just inside the door; a familiar-looking young face with fair skin and long, blond hair. My mouth was dry. It was difficult to swallow.

The woman's weak, questioning smile collapsed.

"Why are you asking about her?" she said.

"She was a passenger coming to this address but left the car just before we would arrive. Since its dark and the weather's so terrible, I was concerned that she got home okay."

The woman's eyes flared with anger and she jabbed her finger at my face.

"If this is your idea of a joke sir, I don't appreciate it. You've got some nerve coming to our home at this hour."

"I'm sorry, I—"

"Don't you think we've been through enough pain all these years without people like you adding to it? Is planning sick pranks like this your idea of fun?"

"I don't understand. What are you talking about?"

Her voice cracked. "You know darn well what I mean. Did someone put you up to this?"

"To what?"

"Making a joke out of our daughter's death."

The last two words struck me like stones. It felt like my heart stopped. Coldness crept up into my torso like a sponge soaking up ice water.

"Death? But I just—"

"You're insinuating that you didn't know that our sixteen-year-old daughter Cecelia was killed on this day thirty years ago?" she said.

The shock must have taken my mind elsewhere for a few moments. The next thing I recalled was observing the woman's lips moving, then hearing her insistent, irate voice rising in volume.

"Answer me, Paul, the cab driver. Are you pleased with what you've done? Now you can laugh about it with your friends. They're likely as depraved as you are."

"No... You don't understand, I—"

"I understand you and your kind well enough." Hate boiled in her eyes.

"Where did this happen to your daughter?" I said.

Her hands curled into white knuckled fists. Her eyes shone with moisture and the veins in her neck reached out. "Near the intersection of Belmont Street and Middle Road, as you well know. She was struck by a hit and run driver on a rainy night like this and died broken and alone in the gutter."

Her words flew into the air, circled like birds, then settled into my consciousness.

"But that's where—"

"People like you are evil." Her words came out like hot nails.

"I'm so—"

"Spare me your fake sympathy," she said, in a mocking tone.

"But I—"

"Do you know what it's like to bury your only child? They never found the driver. It's hard enough for us to get through this day without you coming here and doing this. Have you no humanity or feelings?" She sniffled and tears made tracks in her mascara. "Even decades of passing time can't erase our heartache and loss."

Each word was like a lump of white-hot coal. I tried to explain what happened. "Please let me—"

"Leave our premises now before I call the police," she screamed and then slammed the door.

I sat in the car a long time before driving home. After tossing and turning I drifted off to sleep. The noise of a dripping tap woke me up at 3:00 a.m. It had never interrupted my sleep before. Did I dream of an encounter with a dead girl whose life was absorbed by a city street corner like a sponge and re-animated decades later? Her name and address floated among the jumbled images in my mind. I thought of the hurt on the mother's face. It was all so real. I went down to the cab, turned on the GPS and touched *Destinations* on the menu. The last address was 23 Stone Gate Circle. Things didn't make sense. Perhaps I was going mad.

*

The next day I travelled downtown to the library to access archived microfiche copies of the city newspapers. There it was on the front page of the September 29, 1987 morning edition of the City Examiner:

YOUNG WOMAN KILLED BY HIT AND RUN DRIVER
Cecilia Hanson, sixteen, of 23 Stone Gate Circle in Bennington was struck and killed at the intersection of Belmont Street and Middle Road last evening. There were no witnesses, but police are...

Cece, I think of you often. I could have reached back and touched you that evening—known if you were tangible or phantom. Would your milk-white hand have felt warm and alive in mine, or merely air slipping through my fingers?

I'm sorry you couldn't go home. Wherever you are, I hope you can find peace.

4. DOOR D, ROW TWENTY-TWO

Items were piling up in Ellen's cart. A large bottle of Metamucil, a package of toilet paper, and that special tube of cream for Carl—*Jock Itch* they called the malady that disturbed his sleep. Men sure had some funny things wrong with them. Pharmacies sold everything, now. That large jar of kosher dill pickles was a bargain. Should she buy one or two?

The young woman at the cash register wore green hair and black nail polish. *What a sight. Management shouldn't allow that. Young people are out of control these days. There's no sense of decorum and proper behaviour anymore.*

"But young lady, the sign says fifteen percent off on Seniors Day," Ellen said, after the clerk scanned the Metamucil.

"Yes, on everything except the Metamucil, ma'am. That's already on sale. Do you want me to put it back?"

"No—I'll take it. We're almost out." *Irregularity made Carl grumpy as a bear.*

"There's double points today, ma'am. Need any other groceries?"

"No thank you." Ellen wished the girl would stop calling her ma'am.

"Ice cream is on sale, ma'am."

"It'll melt before I get home. I didn't bring a freezer with me." *What a stupid girl. Why did they hire her?*

"You want bags?" the clerk said.

"Yes, please."

Ellen tapped her card on the terminal and the receipt curled out from a slot on the machine. She inspected it.

"What's this extra ten cents on my bill for?"

"The bags are five cents each ma'am, and you have two."

"Since when are they a nickel each?"

"Ever since the government decided plastic bags are polluting our environment."

Ellen rolled her eyes. *Canada goose poop in the park does too, but they haven't banned geese yet.*

Next stop: the department store.

"If you have a store card, there's an extra five percent off lingerie today," the clerk said.

Ellen quickly extracted the card from her wallet and held it out. "I get the senior's discount too."

"May I see your senior's card?" the young woman said.

Ellen presented it. *The clerk doubts my senior status. That compliment was worth the entire trip.*

"What can I help you with today ma'am?"

Ellen looked around. "I need a brassiere," she whispered.

The girl pointed to a display rack. "These bras are nice. We just got them in."

Black lace push-up? Only tramps and floozies wore those things.

"I'll have that plain white, regular one. Size 36C," Ellen said.

After window-shopping and trying on two blouses she didn't purchase, Ellen had a corned-beef sandwich, Nanaimo bar, and a large iced tea for lunch. It was time to go home.

The mall was gigantic since the expansion a year ago. So many new stores with strange names that gave no clue as to what they sold. That huge outdoor equipment store was a waste: aisles of sporting goods, hunting gear, camping accessories and other junk for men. They should put another department store in there.

She wandered through two wings of the building before reaching the exit door near the computer games store. *Those young people sitting at the terminals. Why aren't they in school?*

Ellen walked toward the handicapped spot in row twenty-two where she parked her blue Toyota Corolla. The shopping bags were awkward to carry, in addition to a large purse.

She stopped, staring wide-eyed at the empty space where her car should have been. The muscles in her upper body tensed, and her legs felt rubbery. *Oh God—my car's been stolen.*

She took several deep breaths, squeezed the handles of her purse harder and looked all around. Must have gone out the wrong exit.

Ellen walked back to the entrance, shopping bags thumping

against her thighs. A stenciled black letter D appearing above the door verified the location was correct. Her heart was beating faster and her underarms were wet.

She set down the shopping bags and rummaged through her purse for her cell phone. Need to call 911. *Not there. Darn. The phone is on the kitchen counter, charging.*

The store security office was hard to find. Ellen was out of breath and the bags were straining her arms by the time she meandered through three corridors and located it. She should have worn more comfortable shoes.

"I need help," she said to the young, male uniformed security officer standing behind the counter.

"Yes ma'am. What can I do for you?"

"My car's been stolen. Call the police."

"Where'd you leave it?"

"At door D, in row twenty-two, the handicapped spot. I always park there."

The man looked Ellen up and down. "You don't appear disabled, ma'am. If there's no handicapped sign on your dash, they'll tow the car away."

"I have a sign on the dash of my car. My legs hurt if I stand too much. My doctor gave me a note so I could get one."

The guard's gaze dropped to her feet. "You really should wear flat shoes or at least orthopedic inserts."

Since when is he an expert on women's shoes or podiatry? "Can we focus on my vehicle, not my feet, please? My car's been stolen. Call the police."

"Maybe you left your car in another spot. It happens a lot. People forget where they park all the time, ma'am."

The nerve of him. "I know where I left it—at door D, row twenty-two, the handicapped spot."

He held up his palm. "Okay ma'am, just relax."

"That's easy for you to say, but it's impossible to be relaxed when your car's been stolen." Ellen held up her key. "How can someone steal a car without having a key to it?"

"You'd be surprised what crooks can do these days, ma'am."

Ellen crossed her arms over her chest. "My name is Ellen, not ma'am if you don't mind."

"Sorry ma'am—I mean Ellen."

Ellen recalled walking through Wal-Mart. That woman in the housewares aisle with the tattooed arms, purple hair and piercings through her ears, bottom lip and nose looked suspicious. Did she steal the car?

"We need to call the police, young man. The longer we delay, the farther away the thieves will get."

"Please calm down ma'am. Why don't we look around first, just to be sure?"

Ellen was tired of being called ma'am by everybody.

"What kind of car was it, ma'am?"

She sighed. "A blue Corolla. The plate says *BESTLADY*."

He flashed a wide smile. "Hey—that's cute."

"It was my husband's idea. I didn't want to spend extra money on a vanity licence plate, but he said it would be cool. His plate says *CARLSCAR*"

They walked to the parking lot outside door D and found row twenty-two. Empty, except for a crumpled fast food bag a seagull was pulling at.

"You're right, lady. There's no car here."

Any fool can see that. How secure do these young, uneducated security guards make the mall, anyway? With nincompoops like him in charge, we wouldn't stand a chance against those terrorists.

"I told you that. My car's not here because it's been stolen. Call the police."

"Why don't we take my car and drive around to the other entrances. You might have left it near one of those by mistake."

Doesn't he listen? "No, I always park right here at door D."

"Let's try the other areas just in case. I'll help you with your bags."

"No—it's okay, I—"

Why did that bag have to rip as soon as he took it?

The guard picked up the items, turned the container of laxative over in his hand and smiled. "Metamucil and toilet paper. Well, they do kind of go together, eh ma'am?"

Ellen could feel her face flush. Adult diapers would have been more embarrassing. *Why does he have to smirk like that?* She let him carry the bags to his car—the pickles were heavy and she was happy she'd only bought one jar. Sitting at the back of the security car didn't appeal to her—it would look as if she was being taken away in custody. Lunch was sitting like a lump in her stomach.

Ellen opened the front passenger door. "I'll sit beside you, young man."

He shrugged. "If you wish, ma'am."

She entered and he pulled away. *My God—does he have to drive like a maniac?*

"Here's row twenty-two, outside door A, ma'am. The handicapped spot has a blue Cadillac in it. That yours?"

Ellen rolled her eyes. "No—I wish."

They drove past a woman pushing a fully stacked shopping cart with one hand and dragging along a screeching boy with the other.

Ellen clucked her tongue. "Look at that. In my day he'd get a good smack. Youngsters aren't brought up properly today."

The young guard glanced sideways at her and then continued circling the mall.

"Here's the handicapped spot in row twenty-two, outside door B ma'am. It's got a yellow Volkswagen Beetle parked in it."

Ellen pushed at the air with her hand. "That's a useless car. We had one forty-five years ago; a tiny trunk for shopping and a puny heater. You'd freeze to death in the winter."

"You should've kept it," he said. "There's a big market for those old Beetles now."

Who cares? Why won't he just call the police?

A surge of panic gripped Ellen as she spotted a neighbour walking out through door B. That busybody Francine Anderson would see her in the car and assume she was arrested.

"Why are you holding your purse up like that ma'am?" the guard said.

"I'm blocking the sun from my face. Too much isn't good for you."

"You should get that sunscreen lotion with SPF in it."

Ellen slouched low in the seat. "Yes—good idea," she said. *Thank goodness Francine didn't see me.*

They continued around to the north door of the mall.

"Here's door C, row twenty-two. A blue car is parked in the handicapped spot, ma'am. That yours?"

"No. Why would I have a vanity plate that says BIGGUY?"

"Yeah, guess you're right. What make did you say your car was ma'am?"

Ellen expelled air through her lips. "A Corolla. C–o–r–o–l–l–a."

"Maybe you parked it in a different row."

What an obstinate fool. "No, I told you that I always park in row twenty-two outside door D. Someone stole my car. Call the police."

"I've got an idea, ma'am. Let's drive up and down the rows. You stick your hand out the window and push the panic button on your key. When we're near your car, you'll hear the horn and we'll find it. May as well use the technology, eh."

"Oh, I suppose." *My God. These young people think they're so smart with all their digital stuff. What a waste of time.*

After fifty minutes of weaving up and down the rows of parked cars while pushing the panic button on her car key, they arrived back at entrance door C. Ellen's hand was numb. No alarm had sounded and she'd dropped her keys twice on the pavement.

"I can't do this anymore young man. I can't move my thumb anymore."

"It's okay. You can stop. We've covered the entire parking lot. Your car's not here."

Ellen massaged her traumatized right hand and raised her voice, "That's because it's been stolen. Do you understand, now?"

He nodded. "I guess we should call the police, ma'am."

Hallelujah. At last it sunk into him.

"I want to call my husband. He'll pick me up," said Ellen.

"Okay, but you'll need to give information to the cops before you leave."

"Yes, of course." She opened her purse and then remembered. "I forgot my cell phone. Is there a pay phone in the mall?"

He pulled a cell phone from his pocket. "Here. Use mine and then I'll call the police for you."

Ellen punched in her home phone number and hit the green call icon.

"It's ringing. Where is that husband of mine?"

He spends all his time in the garage or the basement fussing with car parts. "Carl, what took you so long?...

"That's what I thought. We need to put a phone in the basement...

"Don't tell me to calm down. Something terrible's happened...

"No, I didn't lose my credit card...

"I didn't fall down...

"The drug store wasn't out of your cream, either...

"Yes, yes, I know you need it. Be quiet and listen. Someone's stole my car, that's what happened...

"Don't say no. It's not where I always park. It's gone...

"What do you mean I didn't park it?..."

Ellen's cheeks reddened and she raised a hand to her mouth.

"You have it?"

Her confusion changed to realization, and embarrassment. "Oh—that's right, honey. You dropped me off at door D this morning because you were getting the oil changed in my car. I forgot all about that."

The security guard gaped and shook his head.

Ellen continued her dialogue with Carl.

"Yes dear, I'm ready to be picked up... Right now...At door D...Love you too... Bye."

The guard's knuckles whitened as he gripped the steering wheel. His whole body stiffened. He turned and glared at Ellen.

"I'm so sorry, young man. I don't know how I forgot." Her face brightened. "Well, I guess we won't need the police after all."

The man rubbed his chin, rolled his head, nodded and then pulled at his collar. "Let me guess. That key in your purse is your spare one—right?"

"Yes, I always carry both keys," Ellen said. "I've been known to lock myself out of the vehicle."

He smirked. "I think you've had one of those seniors' moments, lady."

5. A FEW MINUTES TO ETERNITY

"Your appeal was denied."
They told me that a month ago.

Everyone in here's just waitin'
Wonder if anyone out there's thinkin' 'bout me.

I'm kinda famous now. One of the guards told me it was all over the news. That guy's wife was in the paper. She's a widow with two kids it said. "He destroyed our future," she whined.

She meant it was me that did it.

It wasn't me for chrissake. Why would I kill him? I owed him dough, that's for sure. Goddam gamblin' habit. Was into him for a pile o' cash. Little bastard. Placed a coup'la bets in there that day. Thought sure those nags I picked would do it. Fat little bookie boy was walkin' and talkin' when I left.

I remember everythin' the day it all started. That detective Barbarino.

"You're under arrest Lovacs."
"What for?"
"For the murder of Hershel Levine, bookmaker."
"You're crazy. I didn't kill him. You can't pin that on me!"
"You were in his office that day. Your prints were all over the place. His book showed you owed him a lot of money. You killed him to avoid paying, and then robbed him, didn't you?"
"I went in there to lay money on some bets. So, I owed him dough? That don't mean I killed him. Shit! That didn't prove nothin'."
"So where did you get that money they found on you?"
"I won it in a crap game."
"Who else was in that game?"
"Don't know their names. Just a bunch of guys I met."

My trial. What a joke. That prosecutor Carter had it in for me.

"Ladies and gentlemen of the jury, it's an open and shut case. Arthur Lovacs was the last person to see the victim alive, and had the motive to murder him. His fingerprints were there. A woman in the hall saw him leave and said he looked nervous. When he was arrested, his knuckles were cut and bruised. He was unemployed, but had a lot of money in his possession. Mister Levine was a family man. He left behind a widow and two young children."

Told them a hundred fuckin' times I won the money at craps, had a few drinks too many and hurt my hands when I tripped over a curb.

"Ladies and gentlemen, the defendant claims he fell and hurt his hands when he was drunk. He's lying. Look at him. He's a big, strong man. He beat Mister Levine to death with his bare hands and robbed him."

What the hell does my size prove? It's bullshit! Those dicks had it in for me right from the start just 'cause I got a record.

"We have a witness who'll testify he heard the defendant say, *That leech Levine should be squashed like a bug.*"

Just 'cause I said that don't mean I did it. That stinkin' little snitch. He's lucky I'm locked up.

*

What's that sound? Oh—just a door closin'.

Death Row. The gallows room's down there. You could hear the bangin' of the trap door when they were testin' it out. Getting' it ready for me.
Wonder how many guys like me been sittin' here just waitin' t'die. They say the Indian guys in here always start chantin' when someone's takin' that last walk.

Ya notice everythin' locked up in here. Nothin' to do cept' look and listen. Ain't even a window. Everythin' stinks. The whole joint smells of piss and shit. Some jerks still wet the bed. Fuckin' babies.

Food is crap. The guard walks by every fifteen minutes to make sure I'm still here. He never smiles.

"Stop screamin' for chrissake!"
That yellin' at night. Every night, all night. Crazy psychos or druggies outta their heads without a fix.
Never touched that junk.

Everyone's waitin' for midnight.
Cell bars'r cold. The chill creeps up your arms till your whole body's like ice.
Cold. Like the whole fuckin' system.

My trial was quick. That legal aid lawyer they gave me was a prick. Luther Foxcroft. Spent all his time shufflin' papers around. I remember everythin'.

"Admit to killing Levine, Arthur, but tell them you didn't mean to. Say you got into a fight with him and it was an accident."
"Fuck you! I ain't admittin' to nothin'."
"Plead guilty to manslaughter. I'll bargain your sentence down from first degree homicide. You might get out in twenty years."
"I ain't pleadin' guilty to nothin'."
"I'll put you on the stand. You can testify in your own defense."
"Screw you. I'll take my chances."

That screamin'.
"Shut up asshole!"

Carter wouldn't let go.

"Arthur Lovacs has a rap sheet as long as your arm. He's an incorrigible career criminal."
"Objection, your honour. The prosecution's statement is irrelevant."
"Objection overruled, counsellor."
Do ya believe it? The only objection my lawyer made to anythin' was about my long record. Lawyers are all jerks.

"Ladies and gentlemen of the jury, all the evidence against my client is purely circumstantial. The prosecution has presented no concrete evidence that my client murdered Mister Levine."

Foxcroft made a great speech but the jury didn't buy it. They came back with a verdict in less than two hours.

"Ladies and gentlemen of the jury, have you reached a verdict?"

"We have, your honour. We find the defendant, Arthur Lovacs, guilty of murder in the first degree, as charged."

It hit me hard. Guilty of murder one. A big rap.

"Arthur Lovacs, this court sentences you to be hanged by the neck until dead at midnight on December 11, 1962."

Jesus. They're gonna hang me.

"We'll appeal, Arthur. Don't worry. It's not over yet."

"They're gonna kill me! You're my lawyer. You were supposed to get me off."

December 11 was three months away. All that time to sit here and think about them killin' me—think about dyin.' Waitin' to be put down like some dog. Fuckin' lawyer. All he cared about was gettin' his fee.

I scratched a mark on the wall every mornin'. Counted down the days until there was a month to go.

"Your appeal was denied Arthur. They said there was no basis for it."

"Fuck, Foxcroft. You were supposed to get me off."

"I'm sorry, Arthur."

It was a done deal.

It's December 11 today. At midnight it's the end for me. Minutes mean everything now.

What's that? It's not time yet. It can't be time yet.
Oh. Just the guard comin' by.

Wonder what it's like to be dead? What happens to your life?

It's funny. Before you're born there's nothin'. Just a blank. After you enter the world you get this sense of always bein' here. You know it's not true, but your mind plays that trick. Dyin' seems far away and unreal when you're young.

Now it's real. They're gonna kill me and I'll be dead.

I'm scared. I don't wanna die.

All they let me have are these here photos. No other personal items cept' these pictures. Just memories left.

There's my mother. Only decent person in my life. She's young in this one.

There's her and me on my tenth birthday. She made a cake.

I remember her voice.

"Artie. Why are you always getting into trouble? Stealing, fighting and skipping school. Why can't you just be a good boy, study your lessons and play nicely with the other children?"

"Mom—"

"I can't protect you forever. Last week the police were at the door. They'll send you to the reformatory if you keep up like this. You know how upset your father gets when you make trouble."

She died'a cancer when I was in the slammer the second time. Couldn't even say goodbye or go to her funeral.

"You're just like your father, Artie. Lazy and with that same bad temper. Mind me now. It'll turn out no good for you!"

I'm sorry mom. I'm real sorry.

Loathed my father. Hated that I looked like him. Hated what he did to mom.

I can still hear her screamin' and beggin' for him to stop hittin' her. He beat me too. I can still hear the sound of his voice cursin' me.

"I'll teach you a lesson you goddam good for nothin' little bastard. Always causin' trouble. That last lickin' didn't learn you nothin' did it? Guess you need more of the same."

"Who're you to tell anyone what's right? The bottle's the only thing you know. That, and fuckin' every slut in town behind mom's back. You think she doesn't know? You blow all your pay shootin' dice and we don't have enough money to eat proper. When you do come home you're always stinkin' drunk and beat her up."

"You dare talk to me like that. I'll thrash some respect into you, insolent sonofabitch. You're a dumb nothin' and always will be a nothin'. I'm cursed to have a rotten kid like you for a son."

"I can never do anythin' right for you. There's never a kind word outta your mouth for me. You enjoy whippin' me, like you would some dog in the street. You call yourself a father? Fuck you. Go ta hell."

He beat me so bad that time I could hardly walk. Thought he was gonna kill me. Don't know why he didn't. He thrashed me regular 'till that one night when I was fifteen. Grabbed a kitchen knife when he came at me.

"Touch me again you old prick and I'll gut you like a fish."

He must've known I meant it. I was almost as tall as he was.

The fucker left us after that. Good goddam riddance. He shacked up with some whore cross town. Heard she gave him a dose of the clap. He rotted away real slow-like.

Wish I could'a spit on his grave.

Diane…Diane. What did I do to you…to us…?

Wrote a letter to my ex-wife. Don't think I said what I wanted to proper. Can't write my feelin's out very well. Said I was sorry for everythin'.

She prob'ly threw it away without readin' it.

Wonder what my daughter's like now? Hope she turns out good. Wish I had a picture of her.

Jesus, Jesus, Jesus.

Maybe things could've been different for me if I'd gotten a trade and a proper job when I got outta the reformatory. That fuckin' joint was hell. The tough guys'd bugger the young, weak ones and steal their stuff.

Anyone who monkeyed with me got their face smashed.

Too late now. Fuck it all, anyway.

I hear if the hangman does the job right, it'll be quick. The way he sets the rope 'round your neck makes it snap soon as ya drop. When that happens, you're done for.

Y'know, maybe I could do one final thing tonight. Somethin' to screw that hangman. A bit'o revenge, sort of. I could let him have it good—spit in his fuckin' face at the last minute. My hands'll be tied, but I still got my mouth. Yeah! I could gather all the gob together in my cheeks and spit it in the hangman's mug just as I walked onto the gallows. Go out with a bang, eh. They'd write about how I gobbed a big load right in the hangman's face before he dropped me. They'd talk about that for years.

Wonder if I should?

What could he do about it anyways?

What would he do?

Better think on it.

No, not a good idea. That hangman would get even with me. He'd set the rope 'round my neck so's I'd just strangle when the trap door opens. Dyin' wouldn't be quick. I'd only be fuckin' myself by spittin' in his face.

What's that sound?

Not much time left now. God—I'm shakin'.

Gut's upset. Bloody greasy food sittin' there in a lump. T-bone steak with fried potatoes and peas. Chocolate layer cake for desert. Two cokes to drink. They'll give ya whatever ya want for your last meal. Chose steak. May as well have the best, eh?

I'm scared. Don't wanna be dragged in there cryin' and beggin' right up to the end. He's a coward, they'd say.

Gotta be strong. Hold my head up walking in. Haf'ta show 'em I got guts. Showin' courage 'fore they kill me's the only thing I got left. "He died like a man," they'll say.

Oh God—don't let me be weak. I'm scared. Everythin's flashin' by. My heart's poundin'.

Don't think anymore.

What's done is over now.

Jesus Christ I'm scared.

They sent a priest to me a month ago. Father McNamara. Like I care 'bout that religion shit. I remember our first meeting. Funny how things stick in your head. He came carrying a brown paper bag.

"Hello my son."

"What do you want?"

"To offer you fellowship and comfort."

"Did you bring a bottle?"

"That's not allowed."

"How bout' a dame then?"

"There's just me."

"Ahh... you ain't my type."

"I was referring to fellowship in the Lord and the comfort of prayer, Arthur. Will you pray with me?"

"Pray? For what?"

"For forgiveness. If you pray and repent, God will forgive you. Accept our Lord Jesus and redeem your soul."

"Bullshit. There's no fuckin' God! If there's a God, then I'm a pig's ass. I may as well pray to that John over there. Least it flushes when you want it to."

"God exists, Arthur. He created the world and everything in it— you, me, and all living things on this earth."

"Yeah. In seven days—right?"

"That's what it says in the bible."

"I heard somewhere that life came up over millions and millions'a years, not just in a few days."

"Some people believe that evolution idea."

"Not you though, I s'pose."

"I believe God created the universe and that His kingdom and eternal life will be ours. Accept Him, Arthur. Embrace Jesus. He's God's son made flesh through our Virgin Mary. He died for our sins."

"The son'a God coming out of a woman's coozy. What crap."

"Don't deny Him Arthur. He's your salvation."

"Yeah, sure. What a bunch'a hot air. Whaddaya got in the bag?"

"I brought you some things. Magazines, candy, cigarettes and a bible."

"Thanks for the smokes, mags and candy anyway."

"How are they treating you?"

"Okay—for now."

"Tell me about yourself, Arthur."

"My life ain't important."

"Every life has worth in the eyes of God."

"Not much to tell."

"I'd like to hear it anyway."

"Outta school early. In trouble with the law, then reform school. More shit, then prison a coup'la times. Now I'm here waitin' for the end. They're gonna hang me soon. They say I killed a guy."

"I'm sorry, Arthur. You have a family?"

"Not anymore."

"There's no one to visit you?"

"The Sally Ann came round. Brought me a shavin' kit, toothpaste and toothbrush. A guy brings books around. Mostly shit stuff I don't wanna read. No Playboy magazine. Folks'r dead. Was married once. She don't want anythin' to do with me now. Got a daughter somewhere. You?"

"I'm married to the church."

"Oh yeah. No women for you guys—right?"

"It's one of our rules."

"Some bride ya got. No little man in the furry boat, just a pulpit and shoe box closet to hear stupid confessions. No tits ta grab onto, just a rosary. It's funny y'know."

"What is, Arthur?"

"You feel sorry for me 'cause they're gonna kill me and you think I'm goin' t'hell, but I feel sorry for you."

"Why, Arthur?"

"Cause you're whole damn life is just religion, visitin' prisons, lots'a stupid prayin' baloney, and no screwin'. My sufferin's gonna be over soon, but not yours. Ain't that a hoot?"

"All human suffering pales in comparison to Christ's, Arthur. He suffered for all mankind. My life is devoted to service: to God, Jesus and my fellow man. I condemn sin but love the sinner. Jesus said whoever is without sin let him cast the first stone. What I do, is with a glad, willing heart. It's nothing compared to Jesus's sacrifice."

"Yeah, well from where I stand your life is shit, Father. I won't be here for a long time, but I've had a good run compared to you."

"A person lives according to their own conscience. I come in here because a prison is the saddest place on earth and if I can bring one minute of light and comfort into someone's darkness, it's worth it."

"And how do ya know Jesus was such a goody-goody, eh? Maybe He deserved what He got, bein' nailed up on that cross and all. Maybe Him and me ain't that different at all."

"I believe Jesus was the Lamb of God, Arthur—pure and perfect, sent by the creator to wash away all of our sins."

"Sure. And I'm a Girl Guide sellin' gold-plated cookies for a penny. Well, thanks for the stuff anyway. Not many folks come in here to gimme anythin' and the only thing you want from me in return is prayin'."

"Only if you want to."

"I don't."

"Arthur, if you won't pray with me is there anything else I can do for you?"

"Naw."

"Well, goodbye for now, Arthur. I'll pray for you."

"Yeah—thanks."

As he was leavin' I did think of somethin'.

"Wait—Father come back."

"What is it Arthur?"

"I'd like to have a new white shirt with black pants, socks and shoes to wear at my execution. I wanna look decent and not have to wear these crummy lookin' prison clothes I got on now."

Ya should'a seen the look on his face when I asked for those things. He figured I was just a jerk with no dignity and self-respect, not givin' a shit how I looked when I cashed in. Figured he'd flip me off after what I said about Jesus and him throwin' his life away with all that religious stuff, but he didn't.

"That's an unusual request, Arthur. The warden would have to approve it."

"I promise not to cause any trouble 'till the time comes. It's all I'm askin' for. What harm would it do, eh?"

"They have their rules, but I'll ask the warden and let you know. God bless you Arthur. Goodbye for now. You can request for me to come back if you want to talk."

"Sayonara, Father."

I was surprised when Warden Manning approved my request. Thought for sure the answer'd be no. Father McNamara brought me the clothes this mornin'. The shoes are a little tight, but I only got a short way to walk.

Father Mac wasn't such a bad guy for bein' a priest and all. Maybe I was too hard on him. I don't have a mirror, but I think I look pretty good. No belt or shoe laces though. The fuckers'r 'fraid I'll hang myself 'fore they can do it and spoil the show. Ain't that rich?

That priest never gave up on wantin' me to pray and repent, though. He tried again last week.

"Are you Catholic, Arthur?"

"My mother was. Guess that makes me one too, not that it matters any."

"Prayer has the power to heal and comfort. Will you pray with me?"

"Will it heal my neck when they stretch it?"

He gave up on the prayin' thing but wanted to give me the sacraments. Hah. Do ya believe it?

"Father, can I take those pictures of my mother with me in my pocket when the time comes?"

"You were close to her?"

"My mother's the only one who was ever good to me and I gave her grief. I feel bad about that, but looking at her picture makes me feel good."

"She's with Jesus in heaven now."

"You can believe that if you want to, but after it's done I know that I'll never see her face again."

"You can if you believe, repent and ask God for forgiveness and mercy."

"It's sad that she only lives in my memory and when I'm gone it will be like she never existed at all. She was so good."

"All human lives are like that Arthur. Shadows that live when the sun shines, then disappear at dusk. It's what we do in life that lives on after us in this world."

"Then there won't be anything good left from me."

"I'm sorry Arthur. I didn't mean to imply that your life has no worth."

"It's okay. I know what I am."

"I'll ask the warden about the pictures. I'm sure it will be okay."

"Thanks."

"I'll be back… uh, when it's time, Arthur."

"Will you walk with me Father—to the room down there."

"Of course, my son."

He went to go, but then turned back. His face went all funny before he told me. It shook me up. Why didn't he just shut up and keep it to himself. Didn't expect him of all people to turn the knife in my gut.

"Uh... Arthur—there's something I have to tell you."

"What?"

"You might be the last one to hang here. There's been talk about abolishing the death penalty for some time now and a lot of people think it will happen soon."

"Me—the last one? Shit, that's some consolation, father. What a fuckin' honour. Makes me feel real good 'bout them killin' me. Why tell me that now?"

"I wanted you to know that your life, at least at its end, might accomplish some good. Killing is killing. Whether the state does it, or an ordinary person, it's wrong. Your trial and pending execution has received a lot of press and debate recently. When people hear what they did to you, voices will be raised saying enough of this legalized murder. Hopefully no other person will have to suffer this cruel ordeal. Our country will finally become civilized and you will have helped to make it happen."

6. SIDNEY'S RED SUITCASE

Sylvia was annoyed and resolute.

At the luggage store before his business trip to Ottawa, Sidney flinched as his wife picked out a bright red suitcase. It looked like a side of freshly-slaughtered beef with a handle.

Sidney had in mind a genuine leather piece in an elegant designer colour, or a faux alligator model. Something distinctive and fashionable to denote his status as an important corporate traveller—a suitcase easy to spot, but hard to lose.

"That's not a very masculine colour, dear," he said.

Sylvia's eyes flared. "I'm sick of having to replace your lost underwear, socks and shaver," she said, with hands-on-hips determination. "It's exactly what you need. This suitcase will stand out like a beacon in the middle of a black-suitcase ocean. No one will pick it up by accident. Who would want to?"

It was true. He'd lost several suitcases the first year of his new job. Everybody seemed to own a similar black one and other people picked up his by mistake, or it mysteriously disappeared in the bowels of the airline baggage system—a black suitcase disappearing into a black hole. He'd arrive at business meetings without important papers, wearing a rumpled shirt and rancid socks. Appearances were important for career advancement.

Sidney looked around. Her last sentence dented his male pride. "But honey—"

"Look." Sylvia jabbed her finger in his face. "Do you want security, or style when you travel? Practicality is the important thing here, not superficial appearance."

Several remedies had been tried, including affixing the initials *SH* in large duct-taped strips to both sides. Sidney fumed when some wise-guy baggage handler added an *IT* suffix with an indelible marker. He could hear the ripple of sniggers from other travellers as his bag moved around on the baggage carousel.

The tape logo worked for a while until the airport lost the suitcase again—duct tape monogram and all. Sylvia made an orange and green wool pom-pom identifier to tie on the handle of the next suitcase but that one was also lost. Sidney suspected a suitcase conspiracy.

Would having a suitcase with both security *and* prestige be possible?

Before that question could be explored, the hovering clerk, smiling like a retail shark smelling a sale, swooped in for the kill.

"We're having a big clearance event—today only. That suitcase is twenty-five percent off. It's the only one we have left."

Sylvia grinned and pushed the red suitcase toward the woman. "We'll take it," she said. "Give her your credit card, Sidney."

He withdrew the plastic rectangle from his wallet and passed it to her.

Sylvia was bargain-conscious. Normally that pleased him, but not today.

The red suitcase was distinctive, but it wasn't manly. The thought of wheeling it through the airport was mortifying. Already Sidney could feel the flush of embarrassment and hear the amused chuckling of passers-by.

Was he being too macho-sensitive? After all, if the garish red colour kept it from getting lost—it made travelling easier. The discounted price was a bonus. Sidney glanced at Sylvia, beaming with retail satisfaction. The look on her face said it was a done deal. Well, who cared what other people thought?

The long drive to the airport the following Tuesday was more stressful than usual. An accident on the highway delayed traffic. The most convenient parking lot was full, and he forgot his portable tablet. On top of everything else, the meeting was in Ottawa. Hard to imagine the entire country governed from that dull place. Sidney's head ached and his insides were in a knot by the time he walked through the airport entrance door.

There was time to relax and have lunch before the flight. That pretzel and ginger ale snack they'd serve on the plane wouldn't be enough.

One thing he disliked more than airports was airport restaurants. Which hell's kitchen should he patronize this time? It was always an exercise in choosing from a group of equally unpalatable, expensive alternatives. Only the signs out front were different. What would it be today—The Fly By Café, the Chicken Delish, or the Pay and Take

Deli? They'd had chicken for dinner the night before and the cellophane-wrapped sandwiches made with white bread at the deli kiosk looked stale.

Sidney chose the Café.

Placing his luggage on the rack at the entrance, he noticed an identical red suitcase sitting on the right side. What was the chance of that? It probably belonged to a woman. No other man would be cunning enough to have a red suitcase. Sidney set his red suitcase on the left side of the rack and took his briefcase with him.

The only other patron in the café was a man at the counter. The owner of the other red suitcase was probably in the ladies' washroom.

Taking a seat four stools from the other diner, Sidney perused the menu. After several minutes, he glanced around, but the owner of the second red suitcase had not returned. Why did women take so long to do their business?

His inspection of the room caught the other diner's attention. The man smiled at him. It was a peculiar smile, disconcerting, coming from a total stranger. It reminded Sidney of the look the winner in a poker game would have just before he trumped your full house with his four-of-a-kind.

The fellow had a trim, muscular appearance. Did he work out? He was well-dressed with a dark complexion and stylishly-cut, black, curly hair. A diamond stud glinted in his right ear lobe and gold rings of various types adorned his fingers, but no wedding band. One of his wrists bore a heavy gold bracelet and the other an expensive multi-function watch—one of those with buttons and knobs all around the perimeter of the case. The owner was undoubtedly techno-savvy, macho and adventurous—a world traveller, popular with the ladies.

Still no sign of a woman in the cafe. Was it possible his fellow diner was the owner of the other red suitcase? Sidney listened as the waitress took the man's order.

"I'll have smoked salmon on dark pumpernickel toast," the man said, adding, "no crust, lightly toasted, very lightly buttered with a small, side Caesar salad. No croutons and not too much dressing on the salad. Are you using real butter or margarine?"

"Most people want margarine sir," the waitress said, "but you can have real butter if you want it."

"Yes, real butter please."

The man prattled on about the details of his lunch, questioning the garnish items and complaining, using hand gestures, about the myriad poisons found in ordinary tap water. He settled on a bottle of Perrier water as a beverage.

Judging from his fastidious appearance and the methodical, careful way he ordered his meal, this man was a person of discriminating taste. The thought that they might share the same astute foresight to own a red suitcase gave Sidney a feeling of belonging to a select group of discerning, intelligent people. Sylvia had made a wise choice in selecting a red suitcase. Sidney glanced at his fellow traveller, nodded and smiled.

The waitress came over to Sidney with her pen and pad. "May I take your order, sir?"

"I'll have a club sandwich and a large iced tea, please."

"On white or whole wheat?"

"Whole wheat."

"Plain or toasted?"

"Plain."

"Do you want fries and a dill pickle with that?"

"No thank you," Sidney said.

The other diner finished his meal, glanced at his watch and paid his bill before Sidney had eaten half of his sandwich. Did the man inhale his food?

The waitress's face lit up at the credit card transaction. "Thank you very much, sir," she said. The man must have left a generous tip, in keeping with his prosperous appearance.

Sidney watched as he proceeded to the front entrance.

The waitress's voice intruded. "You want anything else sir?" she said.

"Uh, no thank you."

Sidney watched her draw a smiley-face on his bill and place it on the counter. He noticed that the man had left. One red suitcase remained on the rack. His intuition was correct. That fellow was the owner of the other red suitcase; obviously a person of shrewd intelligence, and an original thinker.

Sidney paid his bill and went to retrieve his suitcase. He drew in a rapid breath and stiffened as he came up to the rack. The red suitcase was sitting on the *right-hand* side of the rack, not the *left* where he'd placed his. Had it been moved? Sidney placed the suitcase on a bench. Oh Oh. It wasn't locked.

He lifted the lid. A wave of heat crept up his neck and face as he viewed the contents. Sidney slammed it shut and looked around. No one was nearby. Thank goodness.

He opened it again. Aside from men's boxer shorts, two shirts, black socks and a toiletries case, there was a pair of red, size ten high-heeled ladies pumps. A transparent plastic case held an assortment of women's cosmetics. Touching a pair of panties and a thong buried among the clothing made him queasy. He pulled out his hand and wiped his palm on his jacket. A mesh pouch in the right corner contained a black bustier, fishnet nylons, lace garter, brassiere and long blonde wig.

A brown paper bag on the left was crammed with magazines. Sidney extracted one. A surge of arousal rose in his groin as he flicked through the glossy pages observing men and women engaged in explicit sex acts of every variety. Sidney dropped the magazine back into the suitcase, closed it, sat down, squeezed his legs together and placed his briefcase on his lap. His face felt so hot he thought it would appear sunburned. The owner of the suitcase wasn't in the ladies clothing or cosmetics business. Those items were for his recreation.

"That idiot took my suitcase," he said out loud. A young passer-by toting a backpack glanced at him.

Sidney hurried to the departures hall. His heart raced and perspiration from his upper lip dripped a salty taste into his mouth. One wheel of the suitcase squeaked and seized, making it difficult to pull. His underarms were dripping, and calf muscles were tense. Lunch sat in the pit of his stomach like a brick and the image of Sylvia's irate face crossed his mind.

The huge room was crowded: a tide of rippling humanity carrying and pulling luggage of all colours and description. Sidney scanned the moving faces, looking for the one he remembered. No luck. Thank goodness the financial reports were in his briefcase.

Could the gods of luggage be any more cruel? His first day with something Sylvia insisted he buy and look what happened. Why did he listen to her? He knew this was an age of gender fluidity and libidinal diversity. Sidney wasn't prejudiced—he respected all lifestyles, but why did he, Sidney Handfield, have to end up with someone else's suitcase filled with kinky accessories?

He should have bypassed the Café and settled for the airline's miniscule bag of pretzels. What would he do with this luggage? Turning it in to the airport Lost and Found would involve the completion of numerous forms and raise embarrassing questions and smirks. Taking it home was out of the question.

Yes, it was best to claim the airline lost his suitcase—again. Sylvia would be furious. The suitcase she selected was supposedly immune to every air travel hazard. Women think they know everything. Well, she'd get over it. A visit to the Ottawa Wal-Mart would get him what he needed for this trip.

Everything, including his suitcase would have to be replaced once more, but that stranger would be unhappier when he opened it. He would have nothing to entertain himself with that evening except for a copy of *The Economist*, and a self-help book entitled, *Think Your Way To Wealth*.

Sidney went to the men's room, hid the red suitcase behind a large refuse bin and walked away. An announcement came over the public address system. "Attention travellers. Any unattended luggage in the airport will be removed by airport security."

Sidney imagined the abandoned red suitcase surrounded by apprehensive, heavily-armoured bomb disposal technicians and trained sniffer dogs. It would be amusing to witness their reaction to the titillating, but harmless items when it was opened. Thinking about a burly security guard holding up the black bustier and red thong in front of his snickering colleagues almost made him burst out laughing. Of course, the security guard might be a female. Looking at the black bustier, red thong, men's underwear and socks, she'd be amused for a different reason. Was the owner a man cross-dressing as a female or a female who got her thrills donning men's underwear?

Sidney decided to file a lost luggage report and went to the Lost and Found. The airline never found the luggage they had lost previously, but there would be reimbursement.

"It's never enough to buy a replacement," Sylvia would always complain. She was right.

*

"I need to file a claim for lost luggage," he said to the attendant.

A confused look drifted over the woman's face. "Sir, you should have filed a claim with your air carrier at the office adjacent to the baggage carousel at arrivals, not here at the Lost and Found."

"Uh, the airline didn't lose it."

The confusion on the woman's face expanded. "If the airline didn't lose it, why are you filing a claim for lost luggage? How did your luggage get lost?"

"A man took it when I was in the restaurant."

As the woman closed her eyes and shook her head, the reality dawned on Sidney. His mind had taken a vacation. *He* had lost the suitcase. The airline had no responsibility and there would be no compensation. He felt his face flush with embarrassment. Sylvia would be furious if he told her the truth. "You're worse than the airlines. Both of you will put us in the poorhouse replacing luggage," she'd say.

That red suitcase was more than just a piece of luggage. It was an infallible, reasoned solution to a persistent problem and was conceived by a woman *and* a wife. They were never wrong and if a circumstance indicated otherwise, it must have been because the other half of the marriage had done something to impede the correct result.

"If you think the man stole it, you should file a police report," said the attendant.

The police? Sidney's heart thumped in his ears. He seemed to be standing on quicksand. "I think it was a mistake. We don't need the police."

"If it was taken by mistake, that person might turn it in here. You want to file a report with Lost and Found, not a claim for lost luggage."

"Yes, I just realized that. Sorry," he said, pulling at his damp collar.

The woman sighed and pushed a form in front of Sidney. "Fill this out, please."

Sidney completed the form and handed it back. The required information included the date and approximate time of loss, his name, address, the size, style and make of the suitcase, its contents and identifying marks.

"You say there was no luggage tag or other identifying items, sir?"

"Yes, that's right."

"Makes it difficult to identify. We'll have to open it."

Sidney smiled again at the idea of them opening the suitcase he'd left in the washroom.

"Not funny, sir. Just increases our workload," the woman said with a stern look that reminded Sidney of Sylvia's impatient demeanour. "Do you know how many red suitcases there are out there?"

Sidney didn't think there were that many but didn't argue.

"If it is turned in do you want it held for pickup or shipped to you?"

"I'll be back in two days, but I live a hundred kilometres north of here."

"You'd better take the option for shipment. There's a charge. Give me your credit card number.

Sidney gave her the number and after making notes on the form she passed him a slip of paper. "Here's your reference number. Check back with us when you return."

As Sidney walked to the check-in counter the smile slipped from his face and he stopped. Did the washroom where he left the suitcase have a security camera? What if he was recorded on video? Airport officials might take a dim view of someone abandoning a suitcase in a washroom. It might be a serious offense. Even joking about hijacking an aircraft these days can land a person in jail. They might think he was a terrorist planting an explosive device.

After continuing down the concourse Sidney started to perspire. He stopped and looked back. Perhaps he should retrieve the suitcase and turn it in to Lost and Found. Answering embarrassing questions about the contents would be preferable to arrest and interrogation.

He looked at his watch. If he did that, he'd miss his flight and be late for that important meeting. Sidney glanced around. If they were going to apprehend him, they probably would have done so by now. He couldn't see any uniformed officers in the vicinity or anyone paying any attention to him.

He proceeded to the check-in counter, turning to look behind him several times and scanning passers-by. Did they have plain clothes officers in airports?

"Any luggage to check in today?" the clerk said, as Sidney came up to the desk.

"No," Sidney said, turning to look behind him again.

"Would you like to upgrade your ticket to business class, sir?"

Sidney was about to decline the man's offer when a terrifying sight stopped his breath and made his legs weaken. Two blue-uniformed officers walking along the concourse looked in his direction and pointed. As they changed direction and came closer, Sidney's pulse quickened and his muscles tensed. Images of arrest, interrogation, jail and loss of his job flipped through his mind. His damp shirt clung to his body and he swallowed several times and moistened his dry lips. What would Sylvia say? Why didn't he just leave that man's suitcase on the rack at the restaurant or take it to the Lost and Found? How stupid could he be?

Sidney clasped the briefcase to his chest. He'd have to say something to the officers when they accosted him. Possible responses careened and collided in his head. *It was all a misunderstanding, officer. Someone took my luggage. The suitcase in the washroom isn't mine. Please—I've never been in trouble before. I left it there because…*"

Why were those officers smiling and waving? Sidney turned around to look at the adjacent check-in desk. The clerk was a drop-dead, gorgeous young woman. She smiled and waved back at the officers.

"Hi Natalie," one officer said, a wide grin on his face as he passed by with his companion a few feet away from Sidney.

Sidney held his breath as they walked by and he grasped the briefcase to his body so hard, his biceps hurt.

"Hi guys," she replied with a sultry, inviting voice, red lips curved in a wide smile.

Sidney watched the two security officers walk away and turn a corner.

"Are you all right, sir," the clerk said as he held out a boarding pass.

Sidney exhaled, replied, "Yes," took the boarding pass and then walked as fast as he could to his departure gate.

On the return trip home, he decided to check the Lost and Found to see if his suitcase was there.

"Reference number?" said the attendant at the desk.

Sidney handed him the slip of paper with the number. The young man tapped on his computer.

"Yes, a suitcase matching that description was turned in. It was shipped to your home. Sidney Handfield, 24 Milford Road, Center Vespra. Is that correct?"

"It is. Fast service. That's great. Thank you very much."

Sidney felt good as he wheeled his car out of the parking garage. Another luggage crisis had been averted. He wouldn't have to face Sylvia's wrath and harping for the next week.

"See? Sometimes the airline comes through," he'd say, adding, "They ship it right to your house. That's real service."

God knows what she would have done if he'd lost another suitcase. He'd suggest taking a carry-on but knowing her she'd insist on a backpack. He could almost hear her shrill, adamant voice.

"Oh, no. A carry-on suitcase will have to be put out of sight in the overhead compartment. Someone could take it. You can put a back pack under the seat in front of you. Loop the straps around your ankles so there's no chance of it disappearing while you're asleep."

The image of himself in a tailored suit with that lump perched on his back flashed through Sidney's mind. There would be no point in arguing with her. She'd have taken her bitchy pills as soon as he announced the loss of his last suitcase.

Just before the service center at the half-way point of his journey home, the seeping, viscous dread started in his gut and rose like a putrid, black tide. Sidney took the exit ramp to the service center and stopped. The thought hadn't occurred to him, until now.

How could he be sure that the red suitcase shipped to his house was actually his own and not the one owned by the stranger, the one he'd abandoned in the airport washroom? What if they hadn't opened it, or did so, but shipped him the wrong one anyway? The possibility made him quiver with fear. Sylvia would have accepted it and being the organized, fastidious woman she is, would have opened and unpacked it as she always did when he returned from a business trip.

What thoughts and emotions would fill her mind as she sorted through the risqué clothing and pornographic magazines? Disgust? Betrayal? Anger? All of these? Would she even let him into the house?

"After all these years I find out that I didn't really know you," he imagined her saying with a tear-stained, tortured face.

Explanations jostled in his head like a crowd of men pushing through a door in a tavern advertising free beer. *"It's all a mistake. My luggage got switched with another guy's. He's the kinky one, not me. The airport shipped the wrong suitcase. I never saw that stuff before."*

None of those excuses gave him a comforting feeling. There was no easy way out.

She'd never believe he was a deviate or sexual buccaneer, would she? Or, faced with overwhelming evidence, why wouldn't she?

7. UNDER SIEGE FROM BIODIVERSITY

How could Earl have known that the environment would be so spiteful? He'd never been on intimate terms with the natural world unless squirrels, grey pigeons and scruffy brown sparrows foraging on inner-city streets were considered as such. Aside from going to the zoo on a couple of occasions, Earl was as far removed from nature as one could get. That is, until spring, 2007.

*

"We should buy a place in the country," his wife Mary said, over breakfast one morning.

He wasn't so sure about that.

"It'll be wonderful—wide-open green spaces, fresh air, birds, and a quiet, relaxing lifestyle," she said, with bubbling enthusiasm

That sounded appealing, but he'd heard unpleasant stories about country living—polluted, sulphurous, iron-contaminated wells, problematic septic systems and impassible, snow-clogged winter roads. The city felt secure—the *country* sounded isolated and foreign.

Mary flashed her familiar, reassuring smile. "Don't worry, dear. Many new developments are available in rural areas with modern services. We'll find something."

When someone says, "Don't worry," Earl's tendency was to do precisely that. He was a city boy and always had been—living an asphalt-and-concrete existence, alienated from nature all his life. The idea of country living was a dicey prospect.

Mary wouldn't give up. She found many serviced, rural communities. The ads showed people with smiling faces walking and biking on country trails, canoeing on pristine lakes and proudly holding up large fish. Perhaps it was time for a change. What was Earl so worried about?

After much searching, they found a bungalow set on one-half

acre of land.

"I want it," Mary said. When a woman falls in love with something, you can't argue.

The house backed onto a forest of oak, maple, poplar, and pine trees and the development was fully serviced; quiet country living with all the advantages of the big city. Retail shopping was only fifteen minutes away by car. They took possession in August.

*

That year, summer delivered blistering heat with little rain. Their dwelling was a model home built nine months before and the grass had received no attention—brown and crunching under foot like straw. The weeds were thriving. Earl had never seen so many large, different types. His first job after settling in was to get rid of them.

"I want to buy some Killex," he said to the hardware store clerk.

The man shook his head. "We don't sell that stuff anymore. The provincial government banned the sale of all toxic herbicides to the public." He pushed a spray bottle of liquid at Earl's chest. "Unless you have a golf course, all you can buy is this eco-friendly stuff. It's safe. You could probably drink it."

The word *government* raised Earl's credibility antenna. "But does it kill weeds?"

The clerk shrugged. "Usually."

Not a confident answer, but no other option. "I'll take six bottles," Earl said.

*

Earl sweated buckets spraying weeds in the hot sun. They didn't die and he returned to the store.

"The stuff you gave me doesn't work. The weeds are growing faster than ever," he said to the same clerk.

The man shrugged again. Was that a standard response to customers' concerns?

"What can I say? It's government policy," he said, while reaching for an odd-looking tool. "Try this—it's called a Weed Hound. You put the tines over the weed, push them down with your foot, give it a twist, and pull the weed out in a plug of earth. Just make sure you get the whole root or else it'll grow back."

Earl's muscles tensed. "That's a lot of work. We have a half-acre of property."

The clerk bristled. "It takes effort to preserve the biosphere. We all have to do our part for the environment."

Earl shut up and bought the Weed Hound. After two backbreaking days of effort, he had all the weeds removed—sort of. The long roots usually broke off, leaving some in the ground. Earl heard the remaining buried portion of the weeds saying, *See you again later on.*

They came back, larger than ever and divots from the tool made the lawn all bumpy—like ski moguls.

*

One evening that fall, the radio said the wind was blowing at ninety kilometers per hour. It howled and whistled around the corners of the house, swirling vortices of dry leaves. The tops of the eighty-foot tall pine trees at the back swayed back and forth, taunting Earl and Mary like giant, sneering bullies. The leafy branches of the other trees thrashed around deliriously in the gale-like dervishes.

A crash at 2:00 a.m. jolted them out of bed. A tree on the front lawn had snapped in half and fallen on the house. The next day they called a tree removal service and an arborist turned up.

"I'll inspect the other trees on your property while I'm here," the man said. His verdict: two large poplars in bad condition had to come down.

"What would cause that?" Earl said.

"It could be one, or a combination of insects, bacteria, fungus, parasites and climate. You live in a biodiverse natural environment. These things happen all the time."

"How much to remove the trees?"

"Four hundred for both, extra if we take the wood away."

That, plus removing the already fallen tree and repair to the crushed eavestrough, totalled six hundred and fifty dollars.

"You can tell when the pines die," he said. "The tops turn brown." Was he preparing Earl for more tree calamities?

Earl spent a lot of time looking at the tops of the pine trees surrounding their house.

*

The next spring, they observed a ridge of earth running over the back yard like thick, brown rope.

"What's that?" Mary said.

Earl didn't know, so he called a property maintenance company.

"It's moles digging a tunnel in the earth under the sod," the man said.

"Why would they do that, and how do we get rid of them?"

He shook his head. "You don't get rid of the moles. You get rid of the grubs the moles are going after for food. No grubs, no moles."

"Do you have a poison you can apply for them?"

"No. The government banned them all. You have to use an eco-friendly approach."

That *eco* word again. The government was a pain when they lived in the city. It was even more so in the country. Earl shuddered at the thought of more backbreaking manual labour. "What method would that be?" he said.

"Nematodes."

"Whatatoads?"

"Nematodes. They're a parasite. We spray them on your lawn. They penetrate the soil and kill the grubs."

"I have to pay for parasites?"

"It's bio-symbiosis. Nature used against nature. It's eco-friendly."

Well, at least the man was confident about the remedy.

The cost was one hundred and seventy-five dollars and Earl needed to keep the soil moist for a week afterwards. That spring, one of the hottest on record in their area, made frequent watering of all that grass with portable sprinklers a full-time job. The large water bill arrived later on. Earl wasn't feeling friendly—eco or otherwise.

"Call us if you have any other problems," the man said. "You live in a biodiverse area."

The grubs didn't die. Oh well, the lawn did need aerating.

*

That summer, Earl and Mary planted gardens with flowering plants, shrubs and rose bushes. To enjoy the variety of birds, they purchased expensive feeders mounted on shepherd hooks.

Another crash from the back yard came three nights later. Earl went out to investigate, clad only in pyjamas and slippers. Two large, luminescent eyes greeted him in the dark close to where a bird feeder had stood. The disassembled feeding station lay on the ground and something was feasting on the premium birdseed.

"Shoo!" he said.

The eyes didn't move.

"Shoo!" Earl said, again, waving his hands around and moving closer to the shining eyes.

The eyes moved nearer.

Earl retreated back into the house.

"Why didn't you spray whatever it was with the hose?" Mary said. "Animals don't like water."

Why didn't I think of that? Mary had learned a lot, living in the country.

*

The next morning at breakfast, they watched a squirrel climb up the pole to the hummingbird feeder and drink all the sugary, red liquid.

"It was probably a racoon that pulled down the feeder," said Mike, the hardware store clerk.

Earl had been in the store so often he didn't have to look at the man's name tag anymore.

"You need higher, sturdier poles and guard-cones to keep the animals from getting at them," he said. "It's a common problem. You have a lot of biodiversity here. You may want to consider spraying bear and skunk repellent around."

Another hundred and fifty dollars for poles and cones. Earl didn't dare say anything about the bears and skunks to Mary.

*

Every year, biodiversity delivered a plague to their property. Ants invaded the kitchen most summers. They set ant-traps throughout the house and around it. Griffin, the cat, thought the ones placed inside were toys, and knocked them about with his paws. The squirrels and chipmunks stole all the outside traps if they weren't weighed down with bricks. It was the peanut butter inside that attracted them. With only small holes in the side, how did the rodents get it out? Mary didn't like the brick-secured ant traps.

"The property looks like a clay-brick Stonehenge," she said.

The year after the racoon visit, rabbits proliferated, eating everything in sight including ready-to-blossom flowers, rose and sand cherry bushes, and the entire contents of their vegetable garden except the tomatoes. Rabbits eat carrots don't they? How the heck do they eat plants with thorns? Do their mouths have a steel lining?

"You've watched too many Bugs Bunny cartoons, Earl," Mary

said. "This is the *real* country. Wild animals will eat anything." Yes, Mary had learned a lot.

"Next year I'll enclose the vegetable garden with chicken wire," Earl said.

"Over my dead body. This isn't a farm yard," she replied.

That was the end of their vegetable gardening.

*

The next year brought multiple pestilences. First, hordes of large June bugs crunched under their feet. Mary stayed inside. Then, tent caterpillars took over. They made a feast of the leaves on all the deciduous trees.

Mary looked at the tree branches covered with green, lace doilies. "Aren't you going to do something?" she said.

Earl was afraid to ask Mike the hardware store clerk if he had a remedy for tent caterpillars and considered reminding his wife that they lived in the *real* country but didn't.

"It's biodiversity," he said. "We can't spray the trees."

Earl figured if the caterpillars ate all the leaves, at least he wouldn't have much fall raking to do. It turned out the caterpillars couldn't devour all the leaves, so Earl raked up the same twenty-five bags he always did after cleaning a soggy mess out of the eavestroughs. Fallen leaves, although beautiful in their crimson and gold colouration while still attached to the tree branches, are one of God's make-work projects.

Later that fall, Mary approached Earl with a smile on her face. "I got you something special for your birthday," she said.

"That's nice of you, sweetheart. Thank you. What is it?"

"Next week a man is coming to install gutter guards on the eaves troughs all around the house."

"Uh, that sounds expensive, honey."

"Only twelve-hundred dollars, but money well spent. I hate to see you climbing up a ladder to clean out the eaves troughs twice a year."

"Darling, I'm retired. My labour doesn't come with an hourly rate. You need to save me money, not labour."

Her intentions were good, but Earl still needed to sweep mounds of accumulated pine needles and leaves off the top of the gutter guards every Fall.

Was it too late to move back to the city?

*

One evening the next summer, Mary and Earl were enjoying dinner on the patio under the trees while swishing away annoying insects buzzing around their ears.

Mary pointed up and squinted. "What's that football shaped thing?" she said.

A large wasp's nest dangled from a branch fifteen feet directly above the table. They ran into the kitchen with their dessert. The next day Earl called the pest control company.

"Wasps are very common here," the man said, before spraying the nest and removing it after a stream of the dead creatures cascaded onto their new patio set. Holding it in his hands, he explained how a wasp nest is a fascinating piece of engineering constructed from wood which the wasps chew into a paste.

"Here. See how light it is," he said, pushing it at Mary. She jumped back, scrunching up her face in horrified disgust. Earl was more interested in seeing the bill for removing it.

"Biodiversity," Earl mumbled, after looking at his invoice for one hundred and twenty-five dollars. Later on, they found three more large nests in the trees. The wasps also got in under the soffits and through a space where the gas barbeque line exited the house.

"Nice to see you again," the smiling pest control man said when he returned. Earl noticed he had a brand-new van: the current year's model with all the options. "Business has been very good," he said with a wide grin. That was the year of the wasp plague.

Earl and Mary were now on a first name basis with Bill, the pest control man.

*

It wasn't long before they realized that wasps and bats liked to nest in their closed patio umbrellas so Mary always made Earl open them up while she looked anxiously through the window with telephone in hand, ready to call 911 if they attacked. It is amazing how frightened women are of bats, Earl thought. Do they imagine huge, blood-sucking creatures morphing into Count Draculas? Explanations of how beneficial bats are in controlling mosquitoes were futile. Bats hadn't cost Earl anything—yet.

"I'd rather have the bugs than the bats," Mary said, but did insist on buying an expensive propane-powered mosquito trap. The device generated carbon dioxide and heat to mimic that emitted by human bodies. This attracted the bugs which were then sucked into a vacuum bag. It worked—sort of. Probably the line-up at the trap was too long and some mosquitoes got tired of waiting to get vacuumed in, because Earl and Mary got bitten anyway. Store-bought repellent in a bottle would have been cheaper.

*

A scream from the kitchen startled Earl the following spring. He pulled out his cell phone to call 911.

"Mice are looking in the window," Mary said, after he ran up from the basement.

One was sitting on the window sill munching on something held in its tiny front paws. "Actually, they're chipmunks, dear."

"How do you know?" she said.

"I saw one the other day and searched the internet. It says these are chipmunks.

"You've learned a lot since we moved here," Mary said.

*

During breakfast, lunch and dinner the chipmunks sat on the window sill and stared, unfazed by the presence of Griffin, their large cat who watched intently through the glass only inches away. They made a home under the stone patio and ran across Mary's foot one afternoon when she was sitting out there reading. Earl had never heard his wife shriek that loud before.

"Do something!" she said, face contorted with fright.

Earl wouldn't have survived if he'd reminded Mary that moving to the country was her idea. He called Bill again.

Bill laughed and said, "It's rumoured that chipmunks are going to take over the world."

They and all the other creatures around us, thought Earl. "How can we get rid of them?"

"We have a few options, but not all work well," Bill said. "Methods that do, need to be repeated indefinitely. Their habitat is in the country where you live and they like your birdseed."

"Yes, it's biodiversity," Earl said.

"We can put out traps to poison or electrocute them. Electrocution traps are more humane, but expensive."

Mary crunched up her face. "He wants to kill them? But they're so cute."

Good grief. Now they were adorable—like kittens and puppies. Women were impossible to please.

"What remedy do you have that's not fatal?" Earl said.

"You can spray repellants around. Foxes' urine is the most effective since they're one of chipmunk's main predators, but it's expensive and needs to be repeated every three weeks—more often if it rains."

How do they get urine from foxes? Was that a joke?

"You can spray your own urine around, too. It works almost as well."

That was funny. Mary's face reddened and her eyes flared. "You're not serious."

"Yes, I am," Bill said.

She gave Earl that look and shook her head. "That's not happening if you want to stay married to me. It's gross. Besides, we'll be the laughing stock of the neighbourhood."

Mary, of Dutch heritage, and *Dutch Clean* to boot was adamant. Why was she so upset? He wasn't planning on making a public announcement about peeing all over the garden.

"But honey, I'd apply it with a sprayer."

She shook her head. "No."

"I wouldn't be walking around with my zipper open and everything hanging out. Besides, we'd save money."

"Absolutely not. No urine of any kind is getting sprayed around here. Another one of men's stupid ideas. Just an excuse to drink more beer, that's all."

"Well, you could remove the bird feeders," Bill said. "With no food around, the chipmunks might leave."

Mary groaned. "Then we'd have no birds to look at." Her well-thumbed bird watcher's reference book was at arms-reach on the kitchen window sill beside the breakfast table.

*

In the end, Earl and Mary took no action against the chipmunks. The whole back yard became a network of tunnels like black Swiss cheese and the creatures dug holes faster than they could fill them. Each spring brought out a gang of newborn youngsters frolicking on the stones and chasing each other around in a blur. Mary kept her feet elevated when sitting outside, now, but did enjoy the wide variety of colourful birds that came to the feeders.

The chipmunks didn't cost Earl any money—yet. He wasn't counting all the birdseed they ate.

"Honey, maybe you can train them to eat out of your hand," Earl said one afternoon.

She gave him that look again.

*

The chipmunks weren't mice as Mary first thought, but that didn't mean those rodents were absent. Field mice squeezed under the garage doors, and burrowed into the bags of birdseed, grass seed, and cat food stored on the shelves. Earl found nests built in the corners of the garage where they sheltered from the cold and he had to replace the basement window screens they chewed holes through. He read that they could squeeze through spaces one-half inch wide so he pushed steel wool into all the gaps and covered it with caulk. Earl hoped Griffin the cat might catch them, but the big wuss was afraid of going into the garage. He hadn't told Mary or Bill about the mice. Bill probably had some expensive, high-tech way to get rid of them. Whatever it was, they couldn't afford it.

*

Black squirrels were always running about in the backyard. One day Mary counted eight. Did all the black squirrels in the municipality congregate in their yard for some squirrel summit conference?

They liked to chew the cedar Muskoka chairs. Earl painted them, thinking it would be a deterrent, but it seemed the paint was a condiment that enhanced the flavour, so they chewed on them even more. When not dining on the furniture, they dug in the potted plants, tipped over the birdbath, joined the chipmunks in cleaning up the bird seed spilled from the feeder, and ran along the ledge in front of the windows of the house. If Earl or Mary shooed them away, they climbed a tree and screeched their displeasure at being disturbed.

Last fall, a red squirrel appeared. Their neighbour said they weren't native to the area. It ran up the walls of the house with its jaws stuffed full of leaves, then disappeared over the peak of the roof. Their red, furry visitor was gaining entry to the attic by pushing up the aluminium soffit at the side of a dormer.

Another call to Bill. They had him on speed dial by now.

"It's building a nest in your roof. I'll have to trap and release it far away," he said. "Then you need to get a roofer to brace and securely attach the soffits at the dormers so it can't get in. Red squirrels are rare in this area. Somebody else fifty kilometers away probably trapped it, and then released it here to get rid of it."

Thanks a bunch, friend, whoever you are.

Bill set a baited trap up on the roof near the squirrel's point of entry. "He'll probably be in there by tomorrow morning," he said, with professional assurance.

Earl was delighted to see that red squirrel in the trap the next day. It wasn't moving.

"Dead," Bill said, looking down from the roof. "It got wet from the rain last night and succumbed to hypothermia."

Squirrels are that delicate?

"I'm glad it's dead," Mary said.

Bill's eyebrows lifted and his jaw dropped, shocked at her callous remark.

"Honey, that's mean," Earl said, but echoed her sentiment to himself. That little red terrorist was gone for good. The total for Bill's services and the roof work was nine hundred dollars. That was an expensive squirrel. Later on, Earl totalled up all the money they had spent coping with biodiversity. It would have bought some nice workshop equipment or a riding tractor to cut the grass.

*

Earl and Mary receive a Christmas card from Bill every year. Last December he also sent a calendar with a nature theme. He called Earl this spring.

"I haven't heard from you in a while," Bill said. Earl was sure Bill was anticipating their lucrative patronage would continue this year, as usual.

"Your business card is on the refrigerator. We'll call you if we need anything."

"The emerald ash borer is on its way to this area," Bill said, with an apocalyptic tone.

Earl cringed, anticipating another sales pitch. "What's that?"

"A green bug from Asia that kills trees. I should treat yours to protect them."

Global biodiversity was attacking Earl and Mary with a vengeance now. Earl was afraid to ask the price for emerald ash borer protection. They couldn't afford a second mortgage.

"We'll think about it and get back to you," Earl said. They didn't.

"Why are you sitting there with your head in your hands?" Mary said, after Earl had finished speaking with Bill. "You need to go outside. A bird flew against the window last night and is lying dead on the patio. Green things are croaking in the window wells and something got into our garbage and compost bins. The neighbour said it was a bear. You better call Bill right away."

A profound tiredness descended upon Earl. He looked out the window at the green wall of trees surrounding the house and squirrels cavorting in the yard.

Please, dear God. Spare me from biodiversity.

8. DEATH'S DOOR

Soft, polite tapping at the door; not the fierce pounding which always alarmed her, but change was part of *his* trickery.

Rebecca went to the door, leaned forward and listened, holding her breath. A sound like rustling paper on the other side.

"Who's there?"

"It's Johnnie."

"Johnnie who?"

"Johnnie—from Bigliardi's Grocery. I got your order for this week."

She went to the calendar. Yes, it was his day to come. She'd forgotten, but was it really him out there?

Rebecca returned to the door, pulled a piece of folded paper from her dress pocket and opened it.

"You know what we do next," she said.

"Yeah, I'll read the list out to you, Missus Fraser."

"Read it in order."

"Yes ma'am."

"What's the first thing?"

"A dozen eggs."

"White or brown?"

"Brown, large."

"Go on."

"A loaf of bread."

"What kind?"

"Whole wheat—one hundred percent."

"Right—what's next?"

"A carton of milk."

"What milk did I order?"

"Two percent—white."

"There's more."

"Box of tea—orange pekoe."

"That's correct—what else?"

"Uh, chicken."

"What chicken?"

"Package of chicken legs."

Rebecca stepped back from the door. "No. That's not right. That's not what I ordered."

"Oh—sorry Missus Fraser. My mistake. It should be a package of chicken legs *and* thighs."

The tension in her body eased. "Correct. You alarmed me by saying the wrong chicken, Johnnie. I wondered if it was really you out there."

The voice sighed. "You must know me by now Missus Fraser. I come at the same time each Wednesday."

It sounded like him, but she had to be careful.

"What was my check number this week?"

"Uh…fifty-three."

"How much was my bill?"

"Thirty-four dollars and eighty cents."

"You added your tip and filled in the amount on the check?"

"Yeah—my dad also sent some cut flowers for you."

"No—I can't have any flowers. Take them away."

"Uh, okay Missus Fraser—sorry."

"The last thing is the password Johnnie. Tell me the password."

"It's Eiffel Tower."

"Okay. Leave the bags right next to the door. I'll leave the list for next week's order outside the door, as usual. What about my newspaper?"

"It's in the bag. I put a red elastic band around it."

"Good. You're sure you added your tip to the bill?"

"Yes—three dollars. The total is thirty-seven eighty. Thanks Missus Fraser."

"You're welcome Johnnie. You must be a big boy by now. It's been a long time since I've seen you. How is business these days?"

"I'm in grade eleven now. It's busier than ever at the store. Everyone has'ta eat. Gotta go. Bye Missus Fraser."

Johnnie's footsteps faded on the stairs. Rebecca waited several minutes, released the bolts and lifted the wooden planks from their brackets. She opened the door a crack and peered out.

Two brown paper bags of groceries sat in front of the door. Rebecca swung it open just wide enough to pull the bags in, closed the door, re-secured the locks and replaced the planks. She carried the bags over to a table at the side of the room. The fragrance of cut flowers lingered in her nostrils.

The security of knowing there was food for another week drained the tension from her chest and shoulders.

She remembered the afternoon more than a year ago when she arranged with Johnnie's father to deliver groceries to her basement room for as long as she needed them. It had worked out fine so far, but how much longer could she continue?

Ottavio Bigliardi, the store owner smiled. "No problem Miss Becca. My son'a deliver them'a for you," he said with a thick Italian accent.

Rebecca unpacked the groceries and put them away in a small refrigerator and cupboard.

What did Johnnie look like now? She always gave him a generous tip and made a point of asking about business. He was her lifeline and as the owner's son, dependable, but if business was bad, they might close the store. That would be the end. Thinking about it made her heart beat faster and her palms clammy.

Until Johnnie's next delivery, Rebecca would only have to watch out for her enemy's tricks. He had tried every hoax and connivance imaginable. That one was very crafty—posing as animals, property inspectors, service people, salesmen offering coupons for free items and children selling cookies and chocolate bars for school fund-raisers. Aside from quick openings to take in groceries and sprinkle sugar in the stairwell to keep insects out of the room, the door remained closed, locked, and barricaded.

"I need more vitamins. Next week I should add some cookies to the list. A sweet treat would be nice for a change," she said.

Rebecca sat down and unrolled the newspaper. While reading an article about the latest trend in wedding gowns, she fell asleep, exhausted from the morning's activity.

*

That morning a creature had appeared at the window.

Rebecca peered through the cracks separating the rough boards fastened to the window frame and saw it pacing back and forth. Not the innocent thing it appeared to be.

This time it looked like a kitten. What form would *he* assume next?

It could be anything. There was no end to his deceptions. She struck the boarded window with a stick.

"Shoo! I'm not letting you in. I don't care how starved and pathetic you look. You can't fool me. I know what you're trying to do. Go away."

The narrow slice of figure departed. Rebecca walked from the first window over to the second, then to the door. She checked that everything was in place before turning to sit on the bed and look up at the window.

His animal trick hadn't worked so far. He hoped a momentary lapse of judgement or a tinge of pity for a small creature's pitiful cry or appearance might induce her to open the door.

"You keep trying, but you'll never fool me," she said.

A deep breath. Tension in the muscles of her shoulders and neck eased. A single incandescent light bulb dangling from a wire in the ceiling illuminated the dim, grey, concrete room. Yellow light striking the few possessions in the room cast abstract shadows on the dirty walls. Those black shapes were harmless, familiar companions: the toaster outline, the kettle image, the picture frame wedge, the chair back silhouette and the black fingers of the clothes rack splayed on the wall like a raised, open hand.

She picked up a calendar from the bedside table. Large red letters across the top read: BIGLIARDI'S—YOUR FRIENDLY NEIGHBOURHOOD GROCERY STORE. Another day to mark off.

What did it matter? Each day was the same. The only time that mattered was the present moment. Life was an endless stream of successive moments that held no promise of relief.

The outside appearance of the structure was a dull memory—the colour, material, and design indistinct in her recollection, but she remembered the address—2437 Rosemount Avenue, and the apartment on the fifteenth floor where she lived, number 1512. The concrete tower rising above her was vacant now and glimpses of the empty street in front were all that were visible through the boarded-up windows.

Rebecca knew everything about her concrete room. The room was fifty feet long, twenty-five feet wide and one hundred and seven inches high. She paced the perimeter for exercise: one hundred and fifty feet per circuit, about thirty-five times for one mile. Lately, that much walking made her legs throb with pain and she reduced the circuits to eighteen for a distance of around one-half mile. It would be wonderful to walk outside, but she could only dream about that. She'd forgotten the smell of fresh air. Rebecca didn't consider herself a prisoner. It was her decision to come in to the room and by taking that proactive measure, she evaded *him* just in time. She glanced at the door. They were like gladiators in an arena, but contesting on opposite sides of a metal slab. It was *his* door now, but she could prevent him from entering. That angered him, providing her with a sense of satisfaction and victory.

Life had acquired an economical simplicity since she moved in. Rebecca had made her decision quickly and had little time to prepare. Everything she needed had to be hastily assembled. Meals were plain—cooked on a hot plate or sometimes eaten cold. She washed her few items of clothing in a plastic storage bin and dried them on a line suspended between pipes. Sponge baths from a sink of hot water heated by the kettle maintained basic personal hygiene. The room had cold water and electricity. They had forgotten to turn those utilities off and she was grateful for that. A green toilet and pedestal sink occupied a corner cubicle. Winter wasn't a problem in the temperate state she lived and the below-grade room felt comfortable in the hot, humid summer months. If only she'd brought in an electric fan to circulate the stagnant air.

Vigilance was necessary during waking hours, but especially during the day. Evenings were usually quiet. She wondered why her adversary wasn't more active after dark, but the respite from his harassment was welcome. Solitaire, puzzles, and boxes of used books purchased at the Second Time Around store before she moved in provided entertainment. Some volumes were difficult to understand, but the challenge helped pass the time.

A wind-up clock sluggishly ticked away the minutes and hours. It had stopped once and she had guessed the time when resetting. The exact time of day didn't matter anyway. The small table radio produced only static. Was it broken or was he interfering with the reception?

Rebecca welcomed the newspaper Johnnie delivered each week along with the food—the only communication she had with the outside. The news indicated that the world out there was in a terrible state, but she couldn't be too concerned—the danger on the other side of the door was enough to worry about.

Last week a headline of local news alarmed her so much she couldn't sleep.

CITY COUNCIL TO DISCUSS EAST-SIDE LAND RE-DEVELOPMENT

The area under consideration included the land on which her vacant apartment building stood. If they demolished it, what would she do then? She tried not to dwell on the matter, but it was always on her mind.

Today, a byline in the paper Johnnie delivered brought a smile to her face.

CITY COUNCIL DEADLOCKED FOR EAST-END AREA RE-DEVELOPMENT. CANCELLATION OF THE PROJECT LIKELY

Her building was safe—for now.

How wonderful warm sunshine and a fresh breeze would feel. She used to sit on the balcony of her small apartment watching pedestrians scurrying around like ants far below on the street. The openings between the spaces on the boarded windows reminded her of the world out there: sunlight; an envelope of air that wasn't stale, static and silent; green grass, flowers and trees in the park; other people living carefree, meaningful, active lives. The domain on the other side of the door was a place she once inhabited but going outside was impossible, now.

She made an effort to grasp the simple pleasures available in her drab environment: strips of sunlight moving across the floor as the day matured; a red-orange sunset and the suspended silver brooch of the moon seen through gaps in the boarded windows. It was a way of coping, remaining aware and affirming that life was still worth living. Tiny green shoots of weeds with small purple flowers grew in the window wells. Before coming into the basement room, Rebecca never considered weeds beautiful, but if she ever lived in the outside world again, she vowed never to destroy them.

A silly promise. Being out there again would never happen.

Rainstorms frightened her. Lightning and the booming thunder echoing through the room seemed like the end of the world and when the ceiling light flickered, she feared the permanent loss of electricity. Life would be even harder if that happened. With no light at all, the room would be a crypt.

Rebecca re-read her collection of books. She particularly enjoyed the biography of Dietrich Bonhoeffer, a German Lutheran priest persecuted and murdered by the Nazis. She hadn't known of him before finding that volume in the box of used books but admired his courage in opposing tyranny and brutality in the face of a criminal government. His portrait on the cover flap showed a warm, benevolent, compassionate face—a fellow suffering human being— an inspiration, and reason to keep going.

She felt a kinship with the priest who had been dead for over six decades and kept one of his quotations printed on a piece of paper propped up on her night table.

Silence in the face of evil is itself evil.

Rebecca would never be silent. Whenever that monster came, she screamed at the locked door. He intended to take her life and killing a human being was the most evil thing she could imagine.

She picked up framed pictures of a small boy and a man from the table, caressing the glass with her fingertips, tracing clear lines on the dusty surfaces.

"You were everything. I miss you so much," she said,

She lifted a small, brown, worn teddy bear and pressed the dark nose and strip of faded, red felt tongue against her cheek. Its worn face had small, dark circles where eye buttons had been fastened before small fingers pried them off. A slight smile graced the lips stitched with arcs of yellow thread.

A river of memories carried her to another place and time. The dark room transformed into a small, neat house. A man looked up from his easy chair, newspaper in hand, pipe drooping from his mouth. Her child was in the corner playing with his toys, the little voice conversing with imaginary playmates. His head with the sweet round face, blue eyes, and blonde curls looked up and spoke.

"I'm hungry, Mommy. Can we eat now?"

"Of course dear. Would you like vegetable soup, or the stew I made?"

She glanced over at the kitchen. When she turned back, they were gone. Tears had made wet circles on the bear's head.

Rebecca sat on the bed, motionless and quiet, swallowed by the dark jaws forming the corner of the tomb-like room. She pushed the hanging light and created dancing images on the walls—an imitation of another life, to ease her loneliness, if only for a few moments. Her hips ached and she settled back onto the mattress. Life in the outside world once throbbed with sound and movement. Now there was only silence, stillness, the familiar shadows and the blind, toy bear with its faint smile, clutched in wrinkled, arthritic hands.

*

After two hours, it happened—loud banging on the door. Something could occur at any time, but the intrusion was always a shock, nevertheless. The toy bear slipped to the floor. Ferocious pounding rattled the door bolts and clattered the barricading boards in their brackets.

"You in there. Open up," boomed a male voice.

Rebecca went to the door and leaned forward. "Who is it? What do you want?"

"I'm the City Building Inspector. What are you doing in there? You can't be in this building. It's condemned. Open the door."

"I don't believe you. You're not from the city. I'm wise to your tricks. Go away. Leave me alone."

"Open this door, I said."

"No. Go away."

The coarse voice melted to smooth persuasion. "If you will open the door, I'll show you my identification badge to prove who I am."

"No—I won't open it."

Rebecca watched the knob turn and the force pulling at it from the other side bumping the door back and forth in its frame. She pressed her palms against the cool, steel surface.

The voice hardened and raised in volume. "I'm from the Building Standards Department. You're trespassing. This building's going to be demolished. You have to go—now. Open the door."

"You can't fool me. I know who you are. You're trying to trick me."

"I'm ordering you to open this door immediately."

"Go away."

"If you don't leave right away there's going to be trouble. I'll come back with the sheriff. You're trespassing. I'm ordering you to come out right now."

"No."

After a brief silence, the voice said, "Okay, lady. You'll be sorry—real sorry. I'll be back."

Rebecca kept her ear pressed against the door until the sound of footsteps faded, then picked up the teddy bear and sat on the bed. Today was a day like many others before it: a dreadful existence; long, tedious hours punctuated by intervals of sheer terror; threatening or cajoling voices; deafening noise.

She set the toy upright on the night table, pulled the worn, light cotton dress tightly down over her knees, clasped the threadbare sweater around her body, and rocked her slender frame back and forth on the worn, dirty mattress.

"Tricks. That's all they are—just tricks. He thinks I'm stupid and can be fooled."

Calm filled the room again and the heavy burden of apprehensive, idle time continued.

*

She awoke an hour later. Almost noon. Time to prepare lunch.

A soft knock stilled her hand on the refrigerator door handle. It sounded like Johnnie's tapping, but he never returned after making a delivery. Rebecca moved to the door, leaning forward.

No sound on the other side.

Tapping again. "Hello. Is anyone in there?" a man's voice said. It wasn't Johnnie's.

"Who's there?"

"My name is Richard."

"What do you want?"

"I'm looking for Rebecca Fraser. Does she live here?"

A ripple of awareness caught her. There was something familiar about the voice. Rebecca's brows drew together and her eyes narrowed. "Who wants to know?"

"Richard Fraser—her son. I'm looking for my mother. This building's her last known address. Is she here? Do you know where I can find her?"

Her breath caught in her throat, and heart quickened at hearing that name and recognizing the cherished voice, unheard for so long, yet held deep in the core of memory. Tingling crawled up her neck and goose bumps erupted on her forearms. Could it be him? Was it possible?

"Ritchie…? Ritchie…? Is that you?"

"Mother? Thank God I've found you. Yes, it's me – Richard. I've been searching everywhere for you. Open the door. Let me in."

Rebecca lifted out the barricading boards from their brackets, throwing them to the floor. Hollow thuds echoed through the room. She reached for the sliding bolts, and then hesitated. The cautious habit took control, and the joy slipped from her face.

It might be *him* again, not Richard at all. Rebecca picked up one of the boards and dropped it back into its brackets across the door.

"Mother? What are you doing? Open the door," the voice said.

It couldn't be Richard. He was dead. It had to be *him* pretending to be her son. He'd almost fooled her. A new, cruel trick—diabolical and shrewd. For a moment he had touched a maternal nerve—a longing deep inside her.

"No... No…. You're not my son. You sound like him, but it can't be. He died at sea when the ship sank. All the crew was lost. My son is dead. It's *you* out there."

"Mother—please. It's really me—Ritchie."

What did her adversary really look like when not pretending to be something else? Did he take the form of what he was impersonating in order to lure living things away to oblivion? Did he look like her son or just sound like him?

"Mother? Can you hear me? Please open the door."

"You scheming devil. It's another one of your tricks to get me to open this door. Go away."

"Mother—I don't know what you mean. It *is* me—your son— Richie. I'm not dead. Open the door and you can see me."

"My son died when his merchant ship sank. You're not him."

"I didn't drown. There was a terrible storm and the ship was lost, but a few of us survived. It took me a long time to get back home. When I returned, you were gone and no one knew where you went. I've been looking for you ever since. Please, Mother. Let me in. I love you. I want to see you."

All lies. The black-bordered letter from the Indonesian authorities was in a small wooden box under her bed together with Richard's baby pictures and a lock of his hair sealed in an antique locket. The written words had seared her soul.

We regret to inform you that …

There was no funeral, no body to bury, no last look at him and no closure; only those impersonal, chilling words on a single sheet of paper.

"You think I'm a damn fool. It's another one of your traps. How can you torment me by pretending to be my son who was everything in the world to me? Go away. Leave me alone."

Rebecca's thin body heaved with sobs and she slid down to the floor. She was an empty shell now—drained of health, hope and everything that made life meaningful except for a last spark of the will to resist being pulled into eternal darkness. That voice released a torrent of memories: a precious little boy, a small, neat, white clapboard house, a smiling, loving husband, a past life worth living— all gone now.

"Mother—please."

The imploring resonance of that voice was seductive and earnest. It filled a yearning for something that now seemed more valuable than life. Its appeal was compelling and comforting—irresistible, drawing her like a powerful magnet attracting a sliver of steel.

"Mother…I love you."

Rebecca slapped the palms of her hand on the door and pressed her head against it. "Ritchie…Oh, Ritchie…I love you so much."

She should open the door—end the torment and misery. Only fear, loneliness, and suffering remained in her life. Yes, close her eyes and give in to him. Listen to that wonderful voice of Richard. It would be like going to the beloved boy she missed so much. That sound would swaddle her like a warm cloak in the last seconds of her existence before that monster carried her away. Hearing that last vestige of her boy's voice would be worth it.

"Mother it's really me—Richard. Please let me in."

The urge to go to him lifted her up. She laid hands on the barricading board and raised it an inch from its brackets.

"You're not well, mother. There's no trick. It's Ritchie—your son," the voice said. "I want to take you home with me. I miss you. I love you and want to look after you. The children want to see their grandmother. I've looked everywhere to find you. Please let me in."

A chill crawled through her. Its sharp coldness dissipated the emotion clouding her mind like a breath of frigid air. If he hadn't spoken, she would have opened the door. If he had let silence be his ally, she would have been his, but what the voice on the other side of the door said, and the inflection in the way it spoke, brought her back. No, it wasn't her son Richard out there.

Rebecca released the board and it clunked into the brackets. She wouldn't be carried away by lies.

"No. No. No. I'll never let you in here. You're a horrible fiend. Stop tormenting me. There's no Ritchie, no grandchildren. Ritchie's dead. I know that. I'll never let you get me—never."

The voice tightened; became even, and mechanical. "I'm sorry I upset you Mother. Don't shut me out of your life. Let me help you."

"Go away."

Silence for a few moments.

"I'll leave now and come back again tomorrow. Think about what I said. Let me take you home."

Tears ran down Rebecca's face and she screamed. "No. No. No."

"Goodbye for now, Mother. I'll be back."

"Don't come back here," she shrieked.

The sound of footsteps ebbed away. All became quiet once again. Rebecca pressed the side of her face against the door. The chill of the metal drew the warmth from the side of her head.

"Ritchie...Ritchie...my son. Why, why, why? It's cruel, so cruel."

She replaced the second board into its brackets, pushed at the sliding bolts, then fell onto the bed, drained and exhausted.

*

Rebecca awoke two hours later and walked over to the window. Through the gaps between the boards she could see daylight waning. Her stomach rumbled. Lunch had been missed. An early dinner was soup and toast, but she was too upset to finish it. Rebecca tried to read, but the events of the day intruded, and her eyes didn't progress from the second page of the book to the third.

What would happen tomorrow? Who would he impersonate next?

"My family's all dead," she uttered, as if that statement would be a barrier to future temptation.

Arthritic hands and hips throbbed with pain. Pills would help sleep come. She picked up the bottle of pain killers from the table and lifted the cap. Six tablets were left inside. She wrote the item down on the list for Johnnie.

Slumber didn't come easily that night. Claws scratched at the outside of the door, accompanied by soft whining. He was pretending to be a lost puppy. She ignored the pathetic sounds that rose in volume, then faded and stopped. Cold waves crept up her legs under the blankets. Thoughts were like scalpels peeling back layer after layer of memories.

She pulled out a wooden box from under the bed and opened it. Taking out a locket holding a slip of Richard's hair, she clutched it and slipped back under the covers. The small bauble radiated warmth that percolated up through her arm, across her shoulders and drained down into the core of her body. Starting tomorrow, she would always keep it with her in a dress pocket. If the time came, Rebecca would carry a part of her son with her into the void.

In the distance a dog howled—a lonely, mournful cry. The black ceiling sparkled with dots of moonlight seeping in through gaps between the boards and reflecting off the pots in the kitchen. She drifted off to sleep imagining the dots were stars in a night sky and the mattress a boat drifting on a tranquil, ebony sea.

*

The next day was quiet into the early evening—a welcome respite, but unusual and foreboding. Nothing lurked at the windows or banged on the door. No voices on the other side demanded entry or tempted her with offerings. No incursions of sunlight fell through cracks on the windows. Rebecca's mouth was dry and her legs itched. The arthritic throbbing in her hands and wrists returned. More pills to ease the pain before dinner. Only three left in the bottle now. He tried something every day so it wasn't a matter of *if* he would appear, only *when*. Rebecca glanced repeatedly at the door and up at the windows.

It started before she could release the cap from the pill bottle— dull, distant sounds; unusual, indistinct reverberations.

The disturbance became louder and louder, building bit by bit until it surrounded the room like a crescendo of drumbeats. Sliced shadows darted across the slits of the boarded windows and the sound of angry voices echoed along the walls.

"There he is. Get him," said a male voice.

An orchestra of rough noises at street level—screaming, running feet and banging. Rebecca jumped up from the table and stood in the middle of the room looking alternately at the windows, then the door.

"We'll teach you to come around here," another voice yelled.

A different voice cried out. "No. No. Oh…. Oh…."

The rising tone of an approaching siren. Dashes of flashing red and blue lights crept across the gaps on the boarded windows.

"It's the cops. Scram. We'll finish him off later," someone in the stairwell said.

The sound of running feet receded and the flicker of the coloured lights dissipated. An ominous silence descended. Rebecca waited and listened. She moved to the door, pressing her ear against it. What was that sound?

A small voice moaned in the stairwell on the other side of the door. "Oh….somebody…help me…"

Rebecca held her breath. Her neck and chest muscles tensed. More groans from the stairwell, then the plea repeated.

"Help…help…help…"

"Who is it? What do you want?" she said.

"Help me. I'm hurt," the faint voice said.

"No. Go away."

"They're going to kill me."

"Leave me alone. Go away."

"I've been cut bad."

"I can't help you. Leave me alone."

"I'm bleeding. Help me—please…" The voice was pitiful and urgent.

"You're trying to trick me. Go away."

"Please…."

Rebecca fought rising feelings of sympathy, but each whimper eroded her resolve. Curiosity and empathy for the unseen, youthful voice on the other side of the door built, moan by moan. Each plea tempted her more and more to know what was there.

"Help me. I'm begging you. They'll come back."

She lifted the boards from their brackets on the door, leaned them against the wall and drew back the bolts. The enclosed space of the stairwell gave an emphatic quality to the distressed groaning. She opened the door a pencil width then immediately pushed it closed and slammed the bolts home without looking.

"I can't help you. Go away."

"I can't move. They're coming back to kill me." The plea became more poignant and convincing—a needle, twisting and probing her brain.

Rebecca paced back and forth in front of the door. Her insides tightened. Perhaps she could throw out a bandage or roll out a bottle of water to whoever it was.

No. It had to be like all those times before. Everything on the other side of the door except Johnnie must be ignored, rejected. Only Johnnie could be trusted—if he had the right answers to give, and the voice outside wasn't Johnnie's.

"Lady—please. Help me. I'm bleedin' bad."

Perhaps only a moment's look to assuage her gnawing curiosity. Rebecca retracted the bolts again and opened the door a crack to look out.

A thin, pale boy with blond hair lay in the stairwell, his back against the wall. Blood oozed out of his stomach, between his fingers pressed tightly on the white T-shirt. Wide, blue, imploring eyes stared at Rebecca.

"Don't let me die out here. I'm beggin' you," he said.

Rebecca closed the door again and bolted it. She leaned back against the door, rubbing her face with her hands, then combing her fingers through her hair. Her head swirled and she clasped her shaking body, striving to focus confused and conflicted thinking. He was just a boy—like her son. She should help him, but how could that door be opened and another living thing be let into the room? Impossible. No one could be trusted.

She stared at the dim space of the room. "What should I do? What should I do?" she cried out to the walls.

"You have to help me," the boy called out again.

She screamed at the door and the veins on her neck bulged. "I can't help you. I want to, but I can't. Don't you understand?"

His begging became louder—more pressing.

"Pleeease...help meeeeeee...." The voice became shrill and piercing.

"I can't help you." Why wouldn't he stop? "Go away."

Rebecca covered her ears, but the sound of his voice seemed to careen off the walls, amplifying with each strike on the concrete. She ran from the door to the other end of the room. The agonized pleading followed her, echoing in the rectangular space.

Suddenly it stopped.

She crept back to the door. The beseeching voice started again—only a murmur now. The image of the blond boy lying there helpless was vivid, his life ebbing away. She thought of Richard. If only someone had helped him.

Impulse swept over Rebecca like a wave collapsing a child's sand castle on the shore. She pulled back the bolts, opened the door, dragged the boy into the room and secured it. Struggling, she helped the youth over to the bed.

Her exhausted body trembled. What had she done? Who was he? Would the others come back? Her hands were sticky with his blood. Upon cutting away the blood-soaked T-shirt, she observed two large gashes on his stomach below the tattoo of a young woman with tears running down her cheeks. A puncture in his abdomen would have been more serious. He'd been lucky.

Rebecca tended the youth's wounds, covered him with a blanket and then washed the dried blood from her arms and hands. She pulled a shawl around her shoulders and sat down in a chair alongside the bed, staring at his unconscious face. Her stomach rumbled and she looked over at the kitchen area, but she didn't get up.

Two hours later Rebecca fell asleep. Scratching at the door interrupted the stillness of the night.

*

Soft moaning prodded her awake. Pale light seeped through the gaps between the window boards. It wasn't a dream. The boy was real—lying on her bed with his bandaged upper body supported with pillows. A fine-looking boy—clear skin, golden hair, beautiful hands with long fingers like a musician or artist. What terrible thing had he done for others to want to hurt him?

Her hands itched and she rubbed them together. She could hear her heart thumping in her ears.

His head moved and he groaned.

Rebecca touched his shoulder. "Feeling better?"

The youth's eyes opened, blinked, widened, and then darted from side to side. He stared at the front of her dress soiled with red stains and then tried to rise. His face twisted.

She pushed him gently back down on the pillow. "It's all right. Lie still. You're safe."

"Where am I?"

"In my room. You were hurt and I brought you in."

"They were after me. I was trapped in a stairwell."

Rebecca turned her head and pointed at the door. "Yes—right outside that door over there."

The youth looked at the vertical grey slab and then back at Rebecca. His face was white and flat—the pupils of his eyes dilated to large, brown circles.

"Don't worry. If they come back, they can't get in," she said.

Raising his body again, he grimaced. "Shit. That hurts."

"Don't move around. You have a couple of bad gashes. They're only flesh wounds, but you lost a fair amount of blood. The cuts will be sore for a while, but you'll be all right now that I've sewn them up and bandaged you."

He looked down at his stomach and touched the wrappings girding his torso. "You stitched me up?"

"I used to be a nurse. Still had my old kit with sutures and dressings in it. No antibiotics though. Could've used some alcohol to clean the wounds with."

"Thanks. Uh—when's the doctor comin'?"

"There isn't a doctor coming."

"You called the paramedics instead?"

"I didn't call anyone. There's no phone in here."

"You can go get someone."

"I can't leave this room. There's no one around here for me to get, anyway."

He glanced at the door again. Rebecca saw the fear in his eyes. She sensed what he was thinking. That gang might return at any time. Could they break down the door? Would the boards over the windows keep them out?

"Relax. They can't get in here," she said.

"Who're you, lady?"

"Rebecca Fraser—Missus, but I'm a widow now." She touched his shoulder. "I'll just be a while. Lie still." She walked to the other side of the room.

*

After ten minutes, Rebecca returned with soup, toast and a soft-boiled egg on a tray.

"Here—eat. This will make you feel better."

She sat down beside him and munched on a slice of dry toast.

He picked at the food, glancing alternately at the door, then the windows before pushing the dishes aside.

"You need to eat more to regain your strength, young man. What's your name?"

"Uh—it's Jude."

"How old are you?"

"Sixteen."

"Why'd they hurt you?"

"I crossed onto their turf."

Her forehead creased and head tilted to one side.

"What I mean is that it's their territory. Ya don't go into another gang's area. They'll kill ya. If you're wearin' any of their gang colours they'll chop ya up into little pieces."

Rebecca gasped. Such appalling, senseless violence from people little more than children.

"That's a dangerous chance you took."

"Yeah, you might say that."

"Why'd you come around here then?"

"Just takin' a short cut home." Jude looked around. "Uh, no offense, lady but this place is a dump. I thought old women were neat and clean."

"I used to live up on the fifteenth floor in this building. It was a nice apartment. There was oak parquet flooring and the kitchen had the morning sun. I could eat breakfast on the little balcony. They even sprayed the place for bugs."

"Why'd you move down here into the basement?"

"One day this man came and said everyone had to leave because all the buildings were going to be demolished and this whole area redeveloped into one of those big, new shopping malls."

"Yeah—so what? Everyone knows that. It don't make sense to come down here if the building's gonna be torn down around your head. You should have gone someplace else."

"If I go out there *he'll* get me."

"You got some gangsta guy after you?"

"No, it's not a gang. It's him."

"Jesus lady. What *him* is gonna getcha?"

The colour drained from Rebecca's face and her eyes grew large like a frightened animal.

"It's Death—he's stalking me. He wants to take me."

Jude threw his head back, started to laugh, and then grimaced.

"Ow—don't make me laugh, lady. It hurts my gut too much. You're jokin'—right?"

"No, it's the truth."

"Sure. Now let me understand this deal. You're 'fraid and won't leave here 'cause Mister Death's waitin' outside to kill ya?"

"I'm sure of it. If I go out there or let him into this room, he'll take me. He's very devious. He's tried everything to get in here."

"Death's tryin' to trick ya into lettin' him in here? How?"

"Oh, he's tried every ruse there is. Yesterday he was a starving kitten at the window begging for food. He's come to the door claiming to be the city building inspector, census taker, and meter reader. Last week he posed as a courier with a package. Every day he comes with a different disguise and tries to convince me to open the door. When you were out there yesterday, I thought you might be him."

"Yeah?"

Jude's shirt stuck to his body. Rebecca placed her palm on his forehead. He had a fever.

"How do ya know I'm not the Death man eh? I could be pretendin' to be hurt just to get in here at ya."

"I could see you were badly injured. I touched you and nothing happened to me."

"You're putting me on 'bout Death tryin' to catch ya—right?"

"No. It's true. He's even pretended to be my dead son, Richard. That hurt me the most. I have to be on guard every minute so he doesn't trick me."

"How else does he try to get in here?"

"Sometimes there's a puppy whining at the door, but I know who it really is."

"Yeah? Who?"

"Cerberus."

"Who-a-bus?"

Rebecca's face twitched. She glanced at the door and touched her chest. "It's Cerberus. The three-headed dog that guards the gates of hell. He's Death's bloodhound and sniffs out those marked to die. His master is right behind him."

Jude gaped and his cheek lifted in a crooked smile. "Lady, a dog at the door don't mean nothin'. This area's full'a strays. We throw rocks at em'."

"No, it was really him. I'm certain of it. He scratches all night in the walls too. He's pretending to be a mouse or a rat but I fixed him."

"How'd ya do that?"

"I plugged up all the cracks with steel wool. Rodents won't chew that stuff."

"This area's full'a rats and mice. Maybe you should get a cat to catch 'em."

"What if the cat I bring in is *him* in disguise?"

Jude gave a thin smile. "Mister Death disguised as mice, rats, and cats? Don't forget the spiders, ants, and centipedes, eh."

"Oh, I sprinkle sugar outside the door for the insects so they won't come in this far."

Jude grinned. "Bugs disguised as Death? Yeah—sugar keeps Mister Death outta here, but it can sure kill your teeth." He started to laugh, but his face twisted and he started to choke. Saliva dribbled from his mouth, his face reddened and he clasped his stomach with both hands.

Rebecca stood up. "All this weighs heavily on me and you're making a joke of it," she screamed.

Jude coughed and wiped his forearm across his mouth. He held up his hand. "Uh, sorry. Didn't mean to make fun o'ya. The whole thing just seems kinda unbelievable, y'know."

She leaned closer to him and poked a finger at his face. "Are you insinuating I'm a liar? That's the thanks I get for taking you in here? I took a big risk doing that."

Jude held up his arm. "Uh, I'm grateful. Don't get me wrong, lady. I really appreciate it. Didn't mean ta upset ya."

Rebecca straightened up and glanced over her shoulder at the door. "I can't go in and out just as I please. How would you like to be in my position?"

"No, I wouldn't—that's for sure."

"That's not my door anymore. It's Death's door. If I'm careful, I can keep him out, but that makes him mad, and the longer I do it, the madder he gets. Now he wants to get at me more than ever."

"Yeah—I see. You're in a tough spot here."

"That one can make himself into anything at all. I can't risk bringing a cat in here to hunt mice. They always want to sit in your lap and be petted. Once he touches me I'm done for."

Jude nodded. "Oh—yeah. Good point. I didn't think a'that."

"I've seen him take others and now he wants me. I won't let him take me, though. I don't want to die."

"You saw Death take people? Was he wearin' a black sheet and carryin' a big knife?"

"No, that's the thing, eh. He looks ordinary and fools everyone. I saw him when I was a nurse but didn't realize who it was then. I'd see him come into the hospital pretending to be a visitor carrying flowers and chocolates."

"Really?"

"He'd hug and kiss the patients or hold their hands and tell them they'd soon get better but they died right after he left."

"Maybe it was a coincidence they croaked after gettin' a visitor. They were sick dudes, weren't they?"

"They had operations to make them better. He planned it. Those patients didn't suspect a thing. Children were his favourite disguise. No one can resist hugging a child. Just one touch from him and they were doomed. I saw it happen."

Jude flinched and his face wrinkled. "The death guy dressing up as kids and then snuffin' people? That's crazy."

She drew closer to him, words hissing through yellow teeth and spittle collecting at the sides of her mouth. "I don't like being called crazy."

Jude's face warped with pain and he put his hands up. "I'm real sorry, lady. I didn't mean it like that. It was just a figure of speech, y'know."

Her face twisted into a sneer. "You young people think you know everything, don't you?" The words came out like hot spit. "How come you almost got killed walking home if you're so smart? Tell me that."

He didn't answer right away. She stared at him waiting for a reply.

"Didn't mean any offense lady. What you're sayin' seems unreal, that's all, but if you—"

"Well it's true—all of it."

"Right—if you say so. I believe you. I really do."

"How do you explain the dead babies in the hospital maternity ward then? Some of them would just be born, then die for no reason. Babies don't die just like that. He took them. It was always at night. He'd come in when it was dark, disguised as a janitor sometimes.

Nothing's more evil than killing children."

"Uh, yeah. They're so innocent and all—"

"You can make fun if you want, but I saw it all happen." Rebecca straightened up and the anger slipped from her voice.

"I'm sure you're right, lady. You know what you saw."

"He took my husband too," she said in a sad, quiet voice. "He'd been retired for five months. We were on vacation and the car broke down. The mechanic at the repair shop fixed it, and then shook my husband's hand when he paid the bill. Two hours later my Steve was dead."

Jude's face relaxed. "Jeez. Real sorry ta hear that."

"They said it was a heart attack, but it was really him. That man was dressed in greasy overalls and work boots but he was really Death in disguise. He touched my Steve and he died."

Jude's head sagged. "Just like that, eh."

Tears ran down Rebecca's cheeks, clung to her chin, then dripped onto her lap. "First I lost my son and then my husband." She wiped the back of her hand across her nose and sniffled. "We were so happy, looking forward to our retirement years together. I didn't get a chance to tell him how much I loved him."

"Sounds like he was a good guy."

A thin smile brightened her face. "We had a little white house with black shutters, a verandah and a white picket fence. He made all the furniture in our kitchen."

Rebecca closed her eyes, shook her head from side to side and clenched her fists. "You live together for so many years and take each other for granted. The time flies by and you don't say it. I should have said it. I should have told him how much I loved him."

Jude nodded. "Yeah—guess so."

"That mechanic gave me an odd smile when we left. It bothered me. Later on I realized what it meant. Soon he'd be coming for me too."

"You knew Death was comin' for you?"

"Absolutely. A year later he did."

"How'd ya know?"

Rebecca got up and paced back and forth, gesticulating with her arms and hands. "Every time I went to the supermarket *he* was there disguised as an old woman. She'd always walk toward me in the aisle, smiling. It was the same kind of smile that mechanic gave me."

"You knew by her smile?"

"Yes—don't interrupt. I'm trying to explain it to you."

"Sorry."

"Then one day he was a child who wanted to take my hand and have me help him find his mother. There—do you see it? Do you see the pattern?"

"Uh, not sure."

She threw up her hands. "Are you a fool? It's obvious for goodness sakes. They were his tricks."

"Uh, I see why you had to come in here—smart move."

"I'm all right as long as I don't go outside. The worst part is the loneliness—all day, every day."

"You sure got guts to battle Mister Death. He's a tough customer."

She tapped a bony, crooked index finger on her temple. "You have to think all the time. Stay one step ahead of him."

"You're a clever lady for sure."

"I'll never give up fighting him."

"I can see you're a fighter."

Rebecca pulled her chair closer to the bed and sat down.

"Where do you live, Jude?"

"In the projects with my mother—sometimes. I don't go there much. She's on welfare."

"What do you work at?"

Jude smirked. "My career? Our gang steals cars, breaks them up, and sells the parts."

"Oh," was all she said. He was trapped too—locked in a cage of violence and crime. Rebecca was glad she opened the door and brought him to safety. "You remind me of my son Richard. He was a wonderful boy. What about your father?"

"He buggered off a long time ago."

"Oh."

"Heard he was dead."

"I'm sorry they hurt you Jude, but I'm glad for the company. You're going to feel weak for a while. Stay and rest. You can't walk far in your condition with so much pain."

She touched his forehead with her palm. "Your fever is rising. You should sleep."

"Yeah—guess so."

Rebecca watched him suck in his cheeks. "Are you thirsty, Jude?"

He moved his tongue across his lips. "Yeah. My body's burnin' up and my mouth's so dry it feels like it's stuffed with sawdust."

She jumped up and went over to the kitchen area. "Almost forgot. I need to sprinkle more sugar outside the door to keep the bugs away."

"Yeah. Good idea," Jude said.

She pulled a small knife from the knife block, cut open the top of a bag of sugar and then turned to look at him before replacing it. He seemed to be watching her every move.

"I always make sure to keep plenty of sugar on hand for these bugs," she said.

Jude scanned the dirty sheets he was lying on and lifted the corner of one. He tried swinging his legs over the side of the bed to stand up but fell back grimacing and clutching his abdomen. Cloudy, yellowish fluid stained the bandages and dripped from the bottom of the wrappings.

"Yeah—great idea. No sense in taking any chances, eh?" he said.

Rebecca refilled the sugar bowl. "Those bugs really like sugar. I have to do this every three days."

She went to the door and lifted out the barricading boards, pulled back the bolts, opened the door a crack, and peeked out. Opening the door wider, she quickly spread sugar on the concrete floor of the outside stairwell.

"You got a bottle of beer Rebecca?" he said, just as she closed the door.

She turned around and walked a few steps toward him. "No. You shouldn't drink that stuff. Plain water's better for you."

"How about a can o' Coke then?"

"Don't use it. That stuff's got chemicals in it."

"You got anything in a sealed container?"

"I only have tea bags for tea."

"Okay. Tea's good, but nothing in it."

Rebecca looked at Jude as he lay on the bed rolling his head back and forth on the pillow. He was breathing deeply and she watched his chest rise and fall. He was so much like Richard and memories of her son came drifting back. She'd take good care of him. He was a fine-looking boy. If only he would lead a better life—stop running with a gang and stealing. Young men ate a lot. Johnnie would have to bring extra food.

"I'll make some tea right away. Could use a cup myself. You sure you don't want milk or sugar in it Jude?"

"No—just black."

"Okay."

She went over to the kitchen, filled the electric kettle with water, plugged it in, selected two mugs from the stacked wooden crates serving as a small cupboard, and removed a carton of milk from the little refrigerator.

"I can't drink my tea like you do, Jude. It's too insipid without milk and sugar."

She watched him pull himself up and grimace with pain.

"Each to his own, eh Rebecca."

She added hot water and one tea bag to the brown pot, waited two minutes, poured two cups, and then carried a steaming mug over to Jude before returning to get her own. As she passed the door on the way back to Jude, a knocking made her jump. She turned to observe the barricading boards leaning against the wall and the door bolts retracted. How could she have forgotten?

A torrent of panic surged through her body. The mug of tea slipped from her trembling hands and shattered on the floor, splashing milky liquid over her feet. She rushed to secure the door, but it started to open before she could reach it.

"Hello—anyone in here?" a man's voice said.

Rebecca screamed, and then slumped to the floor. A small, grey mouse scurried in past the stranger's foot and ran along the wall towards the bed.

*

The voice sounded distant as she came to. "No…oh no…," she mumbled.

"It's okay lady—it's okay. I'm sorry I scared you. Are you all right?"

Rebecca kept her eyes closed. Her body stiffened, waiting for what would come. Images, decades old, flashed through her mind. The thing she had tried so hard to prevent had happened. It was the end. She put her hand in her dress pocket and squeezed the locket containing the slip of Richard's hair as tightly as she could. The edges of the object pressed sharply into the flesh of her palm.

"Are you okay lady? Did you hurt yourself?"

What was he waiting for?

"Lady—are you all right?"

As Rebecca opened her eyes, the face she saw wasn't like she imagined *he* would appear. It was normal-looking: round with a ruddy complexion, and pleasant—concerned, even. Any second now his innocuous appearance would transform into something grotesque.

His face remained unchanged. The man tilted his head from side to side.

"Lady? Do you understand me? Can you talk?"

Rebecca sat up. Nothing about her seemed to have altered. She felt the same as before and the room looked the same. She stared at him.

"Oh—oh. Yes, I'm okay. I'm still here—but I thought—"

"What's your name?" he said.

"Rebecca Fraser."

She drew her arms close to her body and pulled her dress down over her knees. "You didn't do anything to me."

The man rose from his crouching position with an indignant look. "Whaddya think I am lady—a pervert? I'm a married man with kids."

He looked around the room again, sniffing the air and squinting into the darkness. "Here—let's get you up on your feet."

Rebecca stood up, hurried over to the door, closed and bolted it, then turned around looking him up and down. It wasn't *him*, but who was he? What did he want?

"Who are you?" she said.

"I'm Henry Davis, the Project Security Manager. Most people call me Hank."

Her face flattened. "What project are you talking about?"

"The re-development plan for this area. The proposal was finally approved by City Council yesterday morning."

Rebecca raised her hands to her cheeks.

Henry squinted into the room again. "The surveyor saw a light in the window so I came to investigate. What are you doing down here?"

"I live here."

His jaw dropped. "What? You can't live here. The whole neighbourhood's condemned. They're going to bring down all the buildings with controlled explosions. The site will be cleared to build a supermall. Didn't you know?"

"I read something about it being put on hold."

"Well, the project's going ahead now. There'll be parking for thousands of cars. All the major retailers will have stores here. There's going to be a fast food joint right here where we're standing."

Rebecca glanced down at the ground then back up at Henry. "I can't leave here."

"Relax. You don't have to leave the neighbourhood. You can live in the seniors' home six blocks away."

"No—I mean I can't leave this room."

Henry waved at her with his hand. "Jesus. You old people are so resistant to change. You're like my mother-in-law. We had her chair re-upholstered and now she refuses to sit in it. Says it's not as good as the old one was."

"I can never leave this room. I'll die if I do."

He pointed his finger at her. "Now look lady. I have my orders. You can't stay here. This building's comin' down soon. You'll be buried in the rubble. The developer'll get fined and the project might be delayed."

Rebecca leaned against the wall to steady herself. Everything had happened so fast. Was he toying with her like a cat bats a mouse around with its paw before crushing its head and devouring it?

"Please—no. Don't make me go."

"I'm a reasonable person. I'll give you until tomorrow afternoon to pack up your stuff and leave. I'll be back at five pm to make sure you're gone."

Rebecca looked around the room surveying her possessions. "No. I can't leave because—"

"If you're still here tomorrow, I'll get the cops and the bailiff. They'll drag you outta here and toss all your stuff into the street."

Rebecca looked at his face bearing a stern expression. It was no use explaining. Jude didn't believe her either.

Jude! She'd forgotten about him. Rebecca looked over at the bed. His mug of tea was on the side table, but she couldn't see him. Of course—he was hiding. A gang member wouldn't want to confront anyone in authority.

"You seem like a nice lady. We don't want to make a scene and cause trouble now, do we?" Henry said.

"No—please. I can't go. It'll be the end of me if I go out there. Don't make me leave this room. Please."

"Lady you can't stay here. I've explained why. Don't you understand?"

She stared past him at the wall.

Henry waved his hand in front of her face. "Lady—do you understand?" He stretched out his arms. "All this is going to be demolished."

Rebecca didn't respond.

"I'll contact Community Services. They'll come and help you move to temporary accommodation. You need to go into an old age home where you can be looked after."

Rebecca's heart raced. Her skin felt clammy and her breathing came in gasps. She could think of only one thing to do and turned to look back into the room.

"Jude. Help me. Don't let him throw me out of here. Make him let me stay. Do something."

Henry looked towards the back of the room, then at Rebecca.

"Who're you talking to lady? Is there someone else hiding in here?"

Rebecca stretched her neck. "Jude—where are you? Say something."

Henry took a few steps back from the door and craned his neck from side to side, scrutinizing the shadowy space.

"Who else is in here with you lady?"

"A boy—his name is Jude. He was sitting over there. Jude—stop hiding. Come out and tell this man why I can't leave here."

"There's a boy in here? Is he related to you?" Rebecca didn't answer.

Henry walked farther into the room and called out.

"Is anyone else here? You have to leave."

There was no answer or sound. He walked through the room, peeked into the toilet cubicle and looked behind a large boiler. He glanced at the bed with boxes stacked at both ends of it. The chair near the wall was empty. He walked back to Rebecca. "I'm not going to leave you, lady. I'll call for help and get someone to come for you right now."

"No—please. I told you I can't leave here."

Rebecca called out to the darkness. "Jude—tell him—please."

Henry pulled a cell phone from his pocket and dialed it.

"Darn, there's no signal down here because of the concrete walls."

He walked over to the door.

"I'm just stepping outside to make a call, lady. I'll be right back."

He unbolted the door, opened it, and then walked out. As he mounted the stairs, Rebecca ran to the door, pushed it shut and fastened it.

"Open the door, lady."

"No. I told you I can't leave here."

The door rattled.

"This won't do you any good. Open up."

"No. Go away and leave me alone."

"It's going to be all right. I'm here with you. No one's going to hurt you. I promise."

"No. Leave me alone."

"If you don't open the door and let me in I'll come back with equipment to break it down."

Rebecca leaned against the door; Henry's pounding on it vibrated through her body. The cold metal drew the warmth from her spine. Head aching and heart racing, she felt weak and wobbly.

"Okay lady. Have it your way." Henry's feet clumped on the stairs, the sound gradually fading to silence.

Rebecca moved from the door into the room. "Jude—he's gone. You can come out now."

There was no answer.

"Where are you Jude? Why didn't you help me—say something to that man or do something? They're coming back to break down the door and throw me out. What am I going to do?"

She looked in the toilet cubicle and behind a storage cabinet near one wall but couldn't find him.

"Jude? Where are you?"

Rebecca swung around in a circle, scanning the dark shadows. "I rescued you when you were hurt. You have to help me. I can't leave here. He'll get me and I'll die. Where are you?"

A squeak emitted from near the bed parallel to the wall and two feet out from it. As Rebecca approached, a mouse darted away from under the bed, disappearing into the shadows at the back of the room.

She went over; pulled away the cardboard boxes stacked at one end of the bed and looked behind it. She gasped, drew back and raised her hands to her mouth. Jude was lying on the floor in the narrow space between the wall and bed, not visible to anyone standing in front.

"Jude?"

She touched his shoulder. The flesh was warm and moist. She placed two fingers on his neck—no pulse. The flesh on his abdomen was black, swollen and covered with blisters. An unpleasant odour invaded her nostrils.

How could he be dead? He was alive only a few minutes before.

She straightened up. A swishing sound turned her around. The atmosphere in the room changed in an odd way. Walls turned and twisted and she had a sensation of sinking, then rising. Breathing was difficult. Thickness settled in her throat, bright lights flashed in her vision and images from the past drifted through her mind. She heard a rattling sound.

A form coalesced from a pool of floating light—a three-dimensional humanoid shape, shimmering and diaphanous with a pale, amorphous face. Moving toward her, its appearance settled into the defined form of a young man wearing white clothing and having long, brown hair and clear, blue eyes. The outline of his body was bordered by a soft aura as he came closer.

Rebecca stared at him. He was beautiful and gentle—unlike anything she had imagined. Her breathing slowed and the sound of her heartbeat faded.

"You've come," she said.

"Yes."

"What's it like?"

"Dying you mean?"

"Yes."

"Do you remember when you were a young child and fell asleep after playing all day?"

"I remember."

"Then your father carried you to bed and the next morning you woke up in your own room, not remembering how you got there?"

"Yes, I remember that too."

"That's what dying is like Rebecca. It's like waking up in another room."

"Is there a heaven?"

Death smiled. "You'll know everything soon." He moved closer and reached out. "Touch my hand, Rebecca."

Her small hand disappeared in his grasp. A feeling of calmness, security and unconditional love infused her.

The door opened and a brilliant illumination flooded the interior of the room, making everything in it appear bright and clean.

They proceeded out through the doorway and up the stairs into the radiant light. The desolate canyon of the city street with its tall, grey, decrepit buildings, abandoned vehicles, piles of rubbish and filthy gutters was gone. Everything was verdant and fragrant. Flowers blossomed and rippled in waves of red, orange, yellow and purple into the distance as far as the eye could see, blending into the horizon. Birds pirouetted and dipped around her head; their songs unlike anything she had ever heard.

Rebecca felt her hand being released and turned to look. Death had vanished. She was alone, but unafraid; feeling only a sense of warmth, liberation and belonging.

In the distance, silhouetted against a silver light, stood a man, beckoning. As she drew closer, he looked familiar.

9. MISTER POLIO

"Oh my God. This is terrible."

Alvin looked up from his Dick Tracy comic book. "What Mom?"

"This article in today's paper."

He went to the kitchen table and looked over her shoulder. The newspaper page displayed several pictures of disabled children. Two boys were equipped with crutches and awkward-looking leg braces and a girl was encased in a metallic cylinder with only her head visible.

His mother shook her head and clucked her tongue. "That poor girl. She's in two prisons: her own body, and that thing they call an iron lung. It's like being canned tuna."

Alvin flinched. "Jeez. She's gotta stay in that thing?"

"Yes, indefinitely. It says here that the machine keeps her alive."

Alvin rolled his shoulders and swallowed to dispel the sour taste in his mouth.

She continued reading the article. "The ominous spectre of polio hangs over the citizens of our city every summer; the scourge of our youth when the days turn warm in late May. This is a particularly bad year. Scientists are working to develop a vaccine, but it is likely years away."

She turned the page to an ad by The March of Dimes Association featuring a picture of their poster boy Timmy, with the caption: DONATE NOW TO FIND A CURE FOR POLIO. A macabre cartoon in the editorial section on the following page showed a girl about to step on a buried land mine labelled polio.

His mother nodded and pointed at the cartoon. "That comparison's perfect. A person never sees the disease until it hits them."

Alvin squirmed. The pathetic image of the girl appearing to be swallowed by that metallic cylinder they called an iron lung, made him shudder.

"It's worse than the war—a stalking enemy you can't see or do anything about," his mother said. "The news on the radio states the toll of polio victims and every week the number rises. Remember the minister's Sunday sermon? He prayed for God to deliver us from it."

Alvin rubbed his neck. It felt like bugs were crawling up around his ears. He hadn't paid attention to the sermon. He hated church, only went because his mother forced him, daydreamed through the service and moved his mouth pretending to sing the hymns which he thought were stupid.

Living a blissful, carefree existence, his interests and awareness had been confined to sports, model aircraft and comic books, but now reminders of polio seemed to be everywhere. *Why hadn't he noticed them before?* The newspaper pictures floating in his mind made his skin creep.

"How do you get polio, Mom?"

"It says here that polio is a virus."

"What's a virus?"

"That's a fancy word for a germ. Germs are everywhere and they can infect you."

"How do you keep from catching polio?"

His mother closed the paper. "Don't know, but germs are why we should always wash our hands before meals." She sighed. "All we can do is trust in God to protect us."

Alvin wasn't sure about his relationship with the Almighty. He had always ignored God and wondered if God did the same to him. He often forgot to wash his hands before meals. Perhaps if he was more diligent about that, polio wouldn't touch him.

After two days, baseball had replaced the spectre of polio in Alvin's mind. That only happened to other kids. He babbled on about Mickey Mantle as he and his friend Calvin walked to the school yard to play catch. Calvin was uncharacteristically quiet.

"A guy I know got sick," Calvin said, in a low, troubled tone of voice as they approached the school.

"Yeah? Who?"

"Billy Burleigh. You don't know him. He goes to another school."

"Sick with what?"

"He's got polio."

The word jarred Alvin. "Holy shit."

"Yeah. Billy's totally paralyzed and in an iron lung."

A scythe of horror sliced through Alvin. The image of that girl in the iron lung washed over him. A friend of a friend had caught the disease. Polio was creeping closer.

"My mom read about it in the paper a couple of days ago," Alvin said. "There was a picture of a girl in one of those things. Why do they put you in that anyway?"

"My Dad says its a machine that makes you breathe. Without it you'll die."

A tremor of apprehension strummed through Alvin. Polio was a germ. He looked at the baseball in Calvin's hand.

"You seen that guy Billy lately—touch him or anything?"

"No. I haven't seen him for a long time."

Alvin wondered if he should play catch with Calvin. *How long did germs last on something? It was Calvin's baseball and he was a friend of Billy's. Had Billy touched the ball?* As they entered the school yard Alvin decided it was probably safe to play catch with Calvin.

That evening, Alvin experienced a terrifying nightmare. He dreamed of being alone in a white room, confined in an iron lung looking at a white ceiling. He couldn't move a muscle in his body or do anything except lie there and look at the lights. A cadaverous, gray-complexioned man in a white coat entered, came to Alvin and touched his cheek with a skeletal hand. His touch was cold, like a concrete wall and a strange sensation crawled across Alvin's face.

"I'm Mr. Polio," the man said, his sunken eyes radiating sardonic pleasure.

"No. Stay away. Don't touch me. I don't want to be in here. When can I get out of this?" Alvin said.

"Never," the man replied, his laughing mouth a black, empty cave.

"But I'm only eight years old. Do it to someone else," Alvin screamed, before waking up.

As the days of summer wore on, Alvin's thoughts about polio receded. Most kids didn't get it. He'd lived for eight summers now. It wouldn't happen to him. The disease and its terrible effects were shuffled to the back of his mind; the images of handicapped children replaced by things he wanted for his upcoming birthday.

"School starts next week. Let's go to the movies," his mother said on a hot, humid Saturday evening in late August 1952. "The theatre is air conditioned."

A welcome treat. Every movement that day made Alvin perspire. Tar in the sidewalk cracks bubbled in the hot sun at midday. Touching the hood of a car would burn your hand. The tiny, noisy fan on the kitchen counter of their flat circulated warm air. Even sitting directly in front of it seemed to provide little relief. As they walked to the neighbourhood movie theatre three blocks away Alvin glanced at the large billboard sign on top of the bank building advertising the March of Dimes. A smiling Timmy, supported by crutches and with braces on his legs, looked down.

The cool interior of the building was a sanctuary after enduring nine days of the record-breaking heat wave.

They saw a double feature including *The House of Dracula* and *The Bride of Frankenstein*. The latter movie was a terrifying story for an eight-year-old child to experience. Henry Frankenstein, creator of the monster, was delirious with excitement screaming, 'It's Alive. It's Alive,' as he revelled in successfully animating the ugly living creature he had cobbled together with body parts purloined from cadavers.

Alvin felt the hair on his neck stand up like the frizzy mop worn by the monster's bride. That grotesque being, together with the thunder and lightning arcing over the dark, brooding Frankenstein castle perched high on a cliff was frightening and Alvin wondered if it would give him nightmares.

When the movies were over, they ventured back out into the sauna-like environment of the August evening, regretting having to leave the cool comfort of the theatre. Encountering the heavy, warm air was like being covered by a thick wool blanket.

As they walked the three blocks home, Alvin felt nauseous and his stomach hurt. *Was it the greasy buttered popcorn and grape Popsicle treats he ate?*

He barely made it to the bathroom before everything came up in a stream of purple mush.

His mother, who sat calmly through the entire ghoulish horror show, now displayed alarm at seeing his condition. Alvin noticed the lines of concern on her face. His father was away on business and she decided there was only one thing to do.

"We have to get the doctor to look at you," she said.

A doctor's visit always meant there would be awful tasting medicine or big horse pills to choke down.

"Why? I feel fine after throwing up," he said.

"We need to make sure it's not p—" She stopped and raised a hand to her mouth. Alvin observed dread in her eyes and saw the blood leach from her face. The realization of what she was thinking pushed him into a vortex of panic.

It might be polio.

The images of those afflicted children flashed by like billboards seen through a moving train window. *What would happen to him now?* He shouldn't have ignored those recent twinges in his joints and muscles. His mother said they were just growing pains, but now he had an ominous feeling that they were much more than that. *He should have been more careful, but how? Perhaps it wasn't such a good idea to share that bag of potato chips with his friend Randy a few days ago. Both of them had put their hands into the same bag. Who knew what germs other kids carried around? Maybe Randy had polio germs on his hands.*

He was in for it. His future, which up to then had been an endless golden thread to be picked up every day, was uncertain. Soon, maybe he wouldn't be able to walk, let alone pick anything up. The thought was like a hammer pounding on the inside of his skull. Images of that iron lung flashed through his mind again and again. He imagined being sealed in one of those metal coffins, enduring a desolate, joyless existence day after day, unable to move a muscle for the rest of his life—a living death.

His heart raced. "It's not polio, is it Mom? It can't be polio," he squealed through tears.

"I'm sure it's not that, honey. It'll be all right." The look on her face gave no comfort. She put Alvin to bed in pyjamas, covered with a blanket. "You need to avoid getting a chill."

Their flat was like an oven and he started to sweat even more. She put her hand on his forehead. "My goodness—you have a fever."

A fever's a sure sign of illness. That never happened to him in the summer before. Alvin bawled louder.

His mother patted his shoulder and then went downstairs. He heard her calling the doctor on the telephone.

Alvin burbled a prayer through his tears.

"Oh please God—don't let it be polio. I'll do anything you want. I'll go to church faithfully from now on; I won't talk back to adults; I'll study harder; I'll do chores without complaining and be real good. Just don't let it be polio."

Until this desperate bargain with God, Alvin hadn't even acknowledged His existence, but now he needed Him.

Strange. He was soaking wet from sweating and crying, but aside from that didn't feel bad at all. In fact, he was getting hungry.

How long would it be before he started to feel sick and become paralyzed? Would his body freeze up gradually, like ice forming on a lake, or all at once like a seized car engine?

He sat up on the edge of the bed and moved his arms and legs around. His abdominal muscles felt tight and sore. *Was the paralysis starting?*

About thirty minutes later, the doorbell rang. Alvin heard two muffled voices downstairs—the agitated, high pitched one of his mother, and the unfamiliar, calmer tone of a man. He held his breath, listening to the sound of footsteps ascending the stairs and approaching his room. The suspense reminded Alvin of a movie he saw where a condemned man walked to his execution.

The door creaked open. "Hello, I'm Doctor Van Delden."

The tall man had a kind, round face framed with golden hair and a pleasant voice. He set his small black bag on Alvin's night table. Alvin's mother hovered anxiously in the open doorway, face wrinkled with worry, holding onto the doorknob with one hand and covering her mouth with the other.

"So, you're not feeling well, eh Alvin?" the doctor said.

Alvin stared at him, his body tense and knuckles white from scrunching the bedcovers with his hands.

"I threw up," he squeaked.

"How many times?"

"Just once—tonight."

The doctor shrugged. "It happens. I did that once after smoking a cigar for the first time."

Alvin liked him right away for his admission but was more concerned with what the doctor was going to discover.

He waved his finger in Alvin's face. "Don't ever smoke young man. It's very bad for you."

Most adults would never admit that. Alvin wanted to try cigarettes. Smoking and drinking beer were the grown-up things to do. His father smoked unfiltered Sportsman cigarettes and drank O'Keefe Ale. *Why did so many adults smoke if it was so bad for you?* Alvin wanted to ask him but didn't. The doctor didn't say anything about not drinking beer.

"Do you have pain anywhere?" the doctor said.

Alvin shook his head and his throat tightened. "It's not polio, is it? I don't want to be in one of those iron tubes," he said in a trembling, high, pleading tone of voice.

The doctor's smile slipped away. "Let's have a look at you."

Alvin's heart sank. He had hoped to hear him say, "No, it isn't."

"He has a fever," Alvin's mother said, her face creased with anxiety.

Alvin gulped. *Having a fever's a bad sign.* His mother said when she was a girl people died of fever.

The doctor removed a thermometer from his bag and placed it in Alvin's mouth. "His temperature is normal."

Alvin exhaled.

"How can that be?" Alvin's mother said. "He's sweating."

"It's summer. The boy doesn't need a heavy blanket and pyjamas on," the doctor replied, before stripping the covers off.

He removed a flat wooden stick and a small flashlight from his black bag. "Open wide and say Ahhhh." He depressed Alvin's tongue with the stick and inspected the interior of his mouth.

"Hmmmm…," he said, frowning.

Alvin stiffened. *What did the doctor see? Did polio make black spots on your tongue?*

His mother edged into the room and her eyes widened. "What? What is it?"

"His tongue is purple," the doctor said.

Her face relaxed. "Oh that. He had a grape Popsicle at the show."

The doctor nodded, and then shone the light into Alvin's face.

"Follow my finger," he said, moving it back, up, down, side to side and in circles. Next, he applied a stethoscope to Alvin's chest and back. "Breathe in and out," he said, while moving the cool diaphragm of the device around on Alvin's warm, clammy skin.

"Can you breathe more deeply, please, Alvin?"

Unease gripped Alvin. *Was the way he was breathing the first sign of polio?*

Alvin took long, deliberate breaths in and out.

"That's better."

After that, the doctor grabbed Alvin's head and moved it back and forth and side to side. "Any discomfort when I do that?"

"No," Alvin replied. It did hurt a little, but the neck pain was from the sunburn he got the day before.

With Alvin's feet dangling over the edge of the bed, the doctor tapped his knee caps with a small rubber-tipped hammer.

"Raise your legs, wiggle your toes and move your feet in circles from the ankles," he said.

Alvin complied.

"Stand up.

Put your arms out to the side.

Wiggle all your fingers.

Move your arms forward and together.

Now move them back.

Arms up over your head.

Now put them down to the side.

Swing them around in circles."

Alvin's arms hurt from the exertion. *Was that a bad sign?*

"Stand on one foot with your hands on your hips and eyes closed."

Alvin almost fell over. *Was polio affecting his balance?*

"Bend down and touch your toes while keeping your knees straight."

Alvin did that and the backs of his legs hurt.

"Walk back and forth across the room heel to toe with your eyes closed."

Alvin bumped into a chair on the way back, stubbing his big toe. It hurt a lot.

"Any discomfort or dizziness?"

"No." Alvin lied. He had felt a little dizzy, but it passed quickly.

"Squat and stand up five times."

The fifth time Alvin almost fell back on his bum.

"Okay," the doctor said, nodding.

Was that a good sign?

Alvin's body dripped with perspiration after performing all those calisthenics and his muscles ached. *Polio affected your muscles didn't it?*

"Lie down," the doctor said.

Alvin reclined on the bed. The doctor raised his legs alternately straight up, then back down. He could feel discomfort when the muscles at the back of his legs stretched.

"Roll over on your stomach." The doctor bent each of Alvin's legs back until the heels touched his buttocks.

"Have you had diarrhea lately?" he asked.

Oh God. Yes. About a month ago when he and Martin stole and ate some green apples from the tree in old man Maranello's back yard. Did that count as a symptom of Polio?

"No," Alvin replied, feeling his face flush in spite of the mask of warm perspiration covering it.

"He's been constipated," his mother said.

"Mom!" Alvin glared at her. His bowel habits were no one's business. *Was constipation a symptom of polio?*

"The doctor's got to know these things," she insisted.

"Oh, we can fix that," the doctor said, smiling.

What did he mean? Was he referring to a dose of that god-awful mineral oil or even worse, an enema? He could worry about that later. Right now polio was the main concern, not pooping.

"How's his appetite?"

"He has two big helpings of everything and several snacks a day," Alvin's mother said.

Alvin's stomach rattled.

The doctor chuckled, reached over and pinched a roll of flesh at Alvin's waist. "I can see the start of a spare tire," he said.

What was so funny?

The doctor replaced his instruments in the black bag and snapped it shut. "I don't see any reason for concern," he said. "Probably just an upset stomach, but if any weakness, stiffness or pain in his joints or muscles develops, call me right away."

Alvin felt the tension in his body melt away like hot wax dripping from a Christmas candle. An incredible feeling of lightness overtook him; a sensation of liberation. All the petty childish annoyances in the days before this evening fell away like dust. The release from fear and worry in the stifling heat was like falling into a pool of cold water. He wouldn't be one of those unfortunate, pitiful, handicapped children impaired in the prime of life with a grim future.

A great tide of relief transformed his mother's face.

"Oh, thank God!" she gushed, closing her eyes, tilting her head up, and clasping her hands together in the attitude of prayer. Alvin saw the tension drain away from her body as if she had just set down a load of clay bricks. She thanked the doctor with effusive gestures several times.

One thought pricked at Alvin. *Would the doctor's lengthy, thorough examination discover something else wrong with his body?* Visions of thick, dark-rimmed eyeglasses, ugly teeth braces and those funny-looking orthopedic shoes his friend Robert had to wear for two years passed through his mind. Well, compared to that iron lung they wouldn't be too bad. Alvin waited for the doctor to say something about that constipation cure he alluded to. Maybe he had forgotten about it.

The doctor pulled out a pad and pencil, and then said to his mother, "I'm going to give you a prescription for him."

Some awful-tasting medicine from the corner drugstore to swallow three times a day, or big horse pills to choke down. Compared to what he'd just endured, it was no big deal. This whole situation was his fault anyway. He'd whined insistently for the popcorn and grape Popsicle treats at the movie theatre. If he hadn't, none of this would have happened. Alvin resigned himself to suffering the medicine-taking consequences, whatever they were.

The doctor walked to the doorway and turned around. "Have a cool bath, young man. It'll make you feel better in this heat."

"Say thank you to the doctor," his mother said.

"Thank you sir." Alvin *was* very thankful. His life, in suspension for a time, had been restored.

"You're welcome Alvin."

Alvin's mother led the doctor down the hallway, thanking him several times again in the process. As they descended the stairs Alvin overheard the doctor say, "The boy could stand to lose some weight. You may want to consider a diet for him."

Would that mean fewer desserts?

It was late and Alvin felt exhausted from the ordeal of the examination. Hopefully his mother would forget about that diet business. He didn't take the doctor's advice about the bath, but sleep came quickly in spite of the heat.

Early the next morning the door to his room creaked open. At first, he pretended to be asleep, but then heard tapping.

"Are you awake?" His mother's head, the face bearing a fretful look, appeared in the opening.

"How do you feel this morning?"

"Okay," Alvin said, after yawning.

"Is any part of you stiff, weak or sore?"

"Don't think so, Mom. Might know better when I get out of bed."

"Stand up and move your arms and legs around."

Alvin did so.

"Well?"

"I feel fine." Alvin's stomach rumbled. It would be nice to have something special for breakfast rather than just the same old toast or corn flakes. Pancakes perhaps.

Before he could ask, she said. "That's good. The doctor left a prescription for you last night."

Alvin had forgotten all about that. "Aw, do I have to?"

"Yes you do. Actually it's for two things."

It was worse than he expected. "Two?"

She smiled, pulled a piece of paper from her dress pocket, unfolded it and read. "It says for constipation, eat cereal with lots of fibre every morning. For upset stomach, no grape Popsicles for three days."

That doctor had a sense of humour. If he played tricks like that on his patients in August, what pranks did he resort to on April Fool's Day? Alvin liked him and hoped that the next time they needed a doctor it would be him that came to the house.

"I'll buy you All-Bran on shopping day," his mother said.

No pills or foul-tasting liquid to gag down was good news, but consuming that cereal was like eating wet, shredded cardboard.

"Mom, on grocery shopping day could you change it to Raisin Bran instead?"

She frowned and shook her head. "I don't think so. That stuff's got less fibre than All-Bran has."

"Please, Mom—please. I'll eat Raisin Bran every morning—I promise. Two bowls even."

She was right. Raisin Bran did have less fibre, but the box always contained a free toy, or something a kid could send away for by cutting out the coupon on the back. The only thing that came with the box of All-Bran was a recipe for making bran muffins. They tasted like dry, roasted cardboard.

After thinking about it for a few moments his mother said, "All right. I suppose some fibre's better than nothing, and you'll be eating it every day. I'll make sure you do. The raisins in it are dried fruit. That's healthy."

On the third day of school, Alvin poured milk on a large bowl of raisin bran. The front of the box displayed cartoon-character bees in flight dropping raisins into a bowl of the flakes. A banner near the bottom announced that a free toy sailboat was inside. Alvin would dig that out after school. A recipe for raisin bran muffins was listed on one side and an offer for a place-setting of four cutlery pieces on the other.

The front page of the newspaper held up by his father showed the mayor greeting Timmy, the March of Dimes poster boy in a drive to raise money to find a cure for polio.

Alvin shivered. Mr. Polio was out there somewhere waiting to grab kids.

That day, at public school, Gloria Mosser, the friendly girl with the long pigtails and bright blue eyes that sat in front of Alvin was absent. She didn't appear for the rest of that week or the next one. The following week the teacher, Miss Secord stood at the front of the room and held up what looked like a large birthday card.

"I want all of you to print your names on this get-well card," she said.

"It's for Gloria Mosser. She has polio and is in the hospital."

10. DEADLINE

The oncologist, his face narrow and flat with thin lips, shook Danny's hand and gestured for him to sit down. The man cleared his throat, opened a file folder and threw him a look that could have caused a bruise.

"I'm sorry to tell you it's bad news," he said.

Danny swallowed and pulled at the damp, sticky collar of his shirt. "How bad is *bad?*"

"You have stage four cancer Mr. Burchard."

"What kind of cancer do I have?"

"Metastatic colon cancer that's spread throughout your body and invaded several major organs."

Danny felt like he'd been slammed against a brick wall. He leaned forward. "You can cure it—right?"

The oncologist shook his head. "I'm afraid not. The prognosis isn't good."

"Can't you operate?"

The doctor shook his head. "The cancer is far too advanced for that, Mr. Burchard."

"What about chemotherapy?" Danny's neighbour, Isabel, had lymphoma and was still in remission five years after her treatments.

The oncologist nodded. "We can try that. It might prolong your life."

Danny wanted to hear the word *save*, not *prolong*. Heaviness pressed down on him. The room seemed to darken and close in.

"It's my obligation to tell you the truth, Mr. Burchard. You're terminally ill."

Danny's leg muscles twitched and he squeezed his hands together. Cold shivers like crawling bugs wriggled up the back of his neck. "You mean I'm going to die?"

"Yes, I'm afraid so."

"But there must be a mistake. I'm only fifty-two."

"I'm sorry," the doctor said in a quiet, sympathetic voice. The tone of finality was unmistakable; the words like dull thuds.

Danny could feel his heart beat and hear the rush of blood in his ears.

"How long do I have?"

"About six months. If you'd come to me sooner, then perhaps...." The doctor jotted on a pad of paper.

"That's all—just six months?"

"Chemotherapy might give you more time."

Danny stared straight ahead, lost in a haze of fear and confusion. He didn't hear the doctor or notice his outstretched hand.

"Mr. Burchard? Mr. Burchard? Daniel?"

The sound of the doctor's voice broke through the wall of his fear. "Oh, sorry—yes?"

"I said chemotherapy may retard the progress of the disease. Take this."

Danny took the small piece of folded paper.

"This is a prescription for medication to manage your pain. We'll arrange more tests and start you on a chemotherapy regimen. The hospital will call with a date for your first treatment."

Danny left the doctor's office. He didn't remember the descent of the elevator or leaving the building. His feet transported him aimlessly through the streets and into a coffee shop.

He scanned the faces at the tables. A group of older men laughed. A little girl, with pink icing from a cupcake all over her mouth, giggled at her mother. A blond woman, her attention riveted to a cell phone, gave a satisfied smile and munched on a muffin while tapping on the device with her thumb. Danny envied their carefree pleasure.

He'd always been a loner, content with his solitude, television shows and books. There was no wife, girlfriend or family in his life to understand what he was going through.

Now, the urge to be in the company of other people was strong. He wanted to sit down with someone and he searched to capture the attention of a sympathetic face, but the anonymous patrons ignored him. Strangers were not inclined to be confidants.

His thoughts pivoted and tumbled, intruded by the random sounds of plates and cups clattering behind the counter, and the voices of employees calling out orders.

"Can I help you," said the attractive, young barista with the flawless, fresh kind of face seen in cosmetic commercials.

Danny wanted to tell the woman who took his order for a coffee and double chocolate donut that he was going to die. Divulging private matters was never his habit, yet revealing this most personal issue to a nameless girl with large eyes who in another life might be his daughter, seemed imperative. Someone had to know—sense what he was feeling.

As she passed him his change, he opened his mouth. Sensing his forthcoming words, she gave a thin smile and waited, but he changed his mind and walked away to a table with one chair.

A murder-mystery novel he once read stated: *The prospect of impending death concentrates the mind.* It was true. He'd never thought about it before, but now, he pondered the matter. What was death like—that event once so far in the future, yet now only a few pages away on the calendar? His senses seemed amplified and keen as a sharpened knife. The thick donut icing had a cloying flavour and texture he'd never noticed before. The drifting tapestry of chatter from other patrons and the aromas of coffee and baking pastry wafting in layers through the air had escaped his awareness until now.

At this moment the simplest things he had barely noticed before seemed beautiful: the afternoon light haloing the head of woman in the corner like a religious figure in a renaissance painting; sprites of steam dancing from the hot, comforting beverage in his hand; clouds like drifting balls of cotton thrown carelessly onto an azure November sky. It was as if his eyes had been exchanged for new ones that could see more acutely.

Nothing else mattered when a person awaited the stroke of death. Objects of great concern only days before were like specks of dust now. What purpose was it all for, this short life which could be taken at any time? Why hadn't he done more; been more aware; tasted more of earthly existence? Dreams and plans previously relegated to an indefinite someday would never be realized, now.

Life's daily activities carried their time constraints, but now he realized that death was the ultimate deadline for everything.

In a strange, ironic way, cancer had set him free to indulge himself in any way he wished. Restraint in anything, or diligent personal habits such as brushing and flossing his teeth three times a day didn't matter now. Danny added three extra packets of sugar to his extra-large coffee and returned to the counter.

"Another double chocolate donut, please," he said to the barista, "and also a dozen of the same to go."

Danny's nose twitched as he entered the cancer treatment center for the first time. The antiseptic odours spoke to him of foulness and decay—not healing and restoration. The cartoonish motivational posters seemed like cruel jokes, giving false hope by spouting clichéd statements such as *Together We Can Beat Cancer.*

He sat down and looked across at the row of waiting patients with pallid, grey faces—men with blotchy skin wearing baseball caps and women with turban-like head coverings and heavy makeup on sunken cheeks which couldn't fully disguise the eroding effects of their illnesses. They stared down at cell phones, fingers poking at inane, inconsequential things or sending vacuous messages. One by one their names were called and the line of ravaged bodies shuffled along like a macabre assembly line. The uncertainty of what would take place over the course of the morning left a knot in the pit of his stomach.

"Daniel Burchard," a firm voice called out.

Danny tensed and caught his breath, jolted by the sound of the nurse's summons.

The woman, with a smile intended as innocent and disarming, ushered him into a large, white-walled room with comfortable-looking reclining chairs.

"How are you today Danny? Have a seat," she said with a forced, superficial cheerfulness.

"Fine," he replied.

I'm not, you silly bitch. You know I'm lousy and dying for chrissake. That's why I'm here. You process dying people, don't you?

A dozen other patients lay prone in chairs receiving treatment. A man looked over at him, gave a thumbs-up gesture and flashed a *I-hit-a-home-run smile.* Danny glared at him and then turned away.

"We need to take your blood for some tests, first," the nurse said.

"Why?"

"To check if your white blood cell count is stable."

Can't they just get on with it?

Danny stared at the ceiling. He felt like an animal, trussed up, about to be put out of its misery. He thought of leaving and telling the doctor to just give him pain-killers until the end came—avoid this degrading, drawn-out attempt to stave off the inevitable.

The nurse came back, hung an IV pack on the stand next to his chair and inserted a needle into his arm. It hurt a lot.

"This is just your pre-med, Mr. Burchard: a cocktail of drugs to relax you and prepare your body for the actual chemo. This will take two hours. After that you will receive two infusions of chemo drugs. Administering each one takes two hours."

Danny clenched his fists and squeezed his eyes shut. He wanted to scream.

The effect of the pre-med drugs was narcotic-like; transporting him to place of warmth and near unconsciousness; a feeling of euphoria, contentment and safety, unaware of the poisons being pumped into his veins.

When the four-hour chemo treatment was over, a black cloud of reality descended. He was neither safe nor well. Danny felt invaded and violated. This was only the first treatment of six.

"They hafta almost kill ya to cure ya," a patient in the next chair said, as Danny waited for his second treatment. Danny didn't want to talk.

Cure? Does this fool really believe he's going to survive?

Bald as a cue ball from the effect of pernicious medications, the stranger rubbed a hand across his white, shiny dome and laughed.

"Look on the bright side. I don't have to cut, comb or shampoo hair now, eh?" he said.

Why won't he shut up? The fellow's stupid guffaw was like stones clattering on a tin roof. Was this the man's pathetic effort at camaraderie and sick-room comedy?

The series of treatments were a degrading, multi-layered medical cake separated by fillings of tests and more tests. Side effects were nausea, bone pain, insomnia, nerve pain, and hair loss. His arms looked like red-dotted pin cushions. A handful of coloured pills preceded each meal; not the kind of appetizers one relished. The variety of hues on the tablets reminded him of the Smarties he liked so much as a child.

As weeks went by, life settled into a dreary routine of travelling to and from the hospital, chemo treatments, and pills.

"You'll have good days, and bad days," the hospital staff said. They were right. Some days he felt well; on others he couldn't walk very far due to the nerve pain in his feet and the time was passed reading, watching television and sleeping.

The apartment became dirty. Mail clogged the compartment near the lobby. Canned foods requiring little preparation were meals. Everything tasted the same. Eating was an effort. The chocolate he once loved, didn't appeal anymore.

The people at work sent a large bouquet of flowers: hot pink roses, orange spray roses, and pink Asiatic Lilies arranged amongst yellow Peruvian Lilies, all complemented by interspersed greenery.

Get well soon, the attached card read.

Danny watched the vivid, attractive blooms gradually wilt, discolour, and shrivel to dry, ochre husks. Watching their slow demise depressed him. They seemed to say, "As we die, so will you."

The garbage chute he tossed them into seemed like an open grave.

The personnel department called to discuss the terms of his sick-leave compensation.

"You'll receive full pay for up to twenty-four weeks, and then go on long term disability at sixty percent of your salary," the benefits administrator said.

She didn't ask how he was doing.

Six months to live and six months full pay? Was that a coincidence?

Friends stopped by with magazines, take-out coffee and donuts—for a while.

"Some people will do anything for a holiday, eh Dan," his co-worker, Jack, said.

Jack wasn't a close friend. Why had he come?

"It's not the type of vacation anyone would look forward to, Jack."

Jack waved away his objection. "Aw, you'll be up and back at it in no time."

"I'm not so sure," Danny said.

"You look good chum," Jack said.

Danny nodded. *It's not true. You're saying that to make me feel good.*

Jack left without a handshake. Did he think cancer was transmitted by touch?

After a while, Danny wished friends would stop visiting. Conversation was awkward and forced. Their eyes bore the same piteous look of the doctors and their silly comments were tiresome and depressing.

Soon, his wish was fulfilled; a landscape of long, lonely, silent days spent in his small apartment. Being cooped up in the confined space was a bleak, empty existence broken only by visits from Arlene, the Meals on Wheels delivery person and Celine, a home-care nurse who visited every other day. One afternoon she passed him a brochure.

"You should consider this while you're mobile, Danny. You're having more bad days now than good ones. It's time."

The cover of the colourful, glossy document read *LIVING LIFE TO THE FULLEST*. The Rose House Hospice was a charity devoted to making the last days of terminally ill people pleasant and comfortable. Danny flipped through the pages and was impressed with the bright, cheerful rooms, open environment, and smiling staff.

The weeks of loneliness and isolation had given him much time to think. Until now he'd lived his life alone. The time left to him might be more enjoyable spent with others in such a place and he would need assistance soon.

"Yes, you're right," he said. The home nurse helped him complete the application. It was accepted.

Danny informed the building's property manager he would leave at the end of the month.

"We need a full month's notice of intent to vacate," the man said.

"But it's only the second day of the month," Danny replied. "You have twenty-eight days to find a new tenant. This apartment building is right downtown. It will rent quickly."

"Those are the rules, Mr. Burchard." He pushed a paper under Danny's nose and pointed to a clause. "This is the lease you signed and those are the terms."

"I'm dying of cancer. There's a vacancy in the hospice and I have to accept it right away."

The manager looked at Danny with cold, impersonal eyes and sniffed. "Well, I guess we'll have to make an exception for you."

"I appreciate it. Thank you."

The manager inspected the apartment and frowned.

"This place is dirty. I'll charge you seventy-five dollars to have it cleaned. If we find vermin, I'll charge you for the exterminator as well."

The man had the personality of a snake trapped in a sack.

"Sorry. I've been sick."

The man shrugged and uttered a dismissive grunt. Danny looked at his stern face and turned-down mouth. *This guy's last job must have been cutting pig's throats in a slaughterhouse. He's treating me like dirt, not a human being. Fuck him. I'm leaving and he won't get another penny from me.*

The world didn't stop for cancer.

Two weeks later, moving day arrived. The treatments had slightly reduced the size of some tumours and the supporting medication made Danny feel well most days. He was glad to hear the doctor say that he could live longer than six months.

He put all his affairs in order. His savings went to purchase a pre-paid funeral including a cemetery plot and gleaming cherry casket. A new blue suit, white shirt and tie would outfit him for the journey into eternity.

His old Ford sedan, not often used, went to Kars4Kids, a charity dedicated to improving the lives of young people. Scratched furniture, books, stereo, CD's and household items were donated to Value Village. The polyester drapes purchased at Wal-Mart years ago went to the old widow down the hall.

Danny looked at the empty apartment. People came into the world with nothing, but accumulated so many possessions during their lives. Now, these things seemed like unnecessary detritus and their removal gave him a rarely experienced, warm feeling of having helped others in need.

His suitcase held only a few items of clothing, two books, and a framed photograph of his dead parents. Soon he wouldn't need even those.

The intercom buzzed. "Taxi," the voice said.

At the doorway, Danny turned to look back into the small apartment where he'd lived for twenty years. He surveyed the worn, oak parquet floor, soiled beige walls, and blue Formica kitchen counter. The place was a cement box in a grey, nondescript concrete obelisk filled with similar cubes, but it had been home. He closed the door and the hollow thud reverberated down the corridor, waning to silence, like something that had expelled its final breath.

A well-dressed, older woman gave a welcoming smile and extended her hand to greet him as he walked into the wide lobby of the hospice.

For a place of final days, it was everything the brochure had described: modern, clean and bright with large windows, wide corridors, sun-filled common spaces, and tasteful furniture. Pictures of outdoor scenes adorned the walls and vases of fresh flowers rested on tables. The air was fresh and non-antiseptic, unlike the hospital wards which reeked of chemical odours.

"Welcome, Danny. I'm Colleen Mason, Director of Rose House," she said. "We're happy to have you here and hope you'll enjoy your new home. Rose House is a place of life and we focus on living well here. We do everything possible to make our guests comfortable. If there's anything you need or have any questions, just ask me, or one of the staff."

"Thank you Ms. Mason."

"You'll share a room with another person," Colleen said. "Your roommate will be Mr. Everett Monteith in room number 512—a fine gentleman. I'm sure you two will get along well."

Danny had forgotten, but now remembered checking the box that gave his consent to share a room with another person.

Had that been a wise decision? What will this roommate be like? A pang of anxiety strummed through him. The decision had been impulsive and out-of-character. He'd lived alone a long time.

She escorted him into an elevator and up to the fifth floor, entering a large room with two beds. One next to a wall was surrounded by a curtain. The fragrant aroma of freshly cut flowers filled the air. Danny sensed the warmth of the space. Artistic pictures and neutral-tone walls illuminated by soft lighting radiated a positive energy. Two small dressers occupied one wall. A television and framed picture of a woman sat on top of one. Floor to ceiling draperies covered an exterior wall, hanging in straight, pleated folds. A pillar of light from the window behind them flowed from the gap between the panels.

"Your bed is beside the window," Coleen said, in a low voice, "Mr. Monteith has the bed beside the wall. He's bed-ridden and it's been one of his bad days. He's asleep."

It had been a long, exhausting day. Danny went to the dining room for dinner. After reading in the common room he took his medication and went to bed early.

The next morning Danny awoke, got out of bed, put on his housecoat, opened the drapes and looked out, squinting against the daylight. He glanced at the closed curtain surrounding Monteith's bed.

He went down to breakfast, deciding to shave later. When he returned, the curtain surrounding his roommate's bed was open and a hand waved at him.

"Well, hello and welcome."

Danny went over.

The deep voice belonged to a tall, emaciated man with sparse, white hair and fine, if gaunt, aquiline features.

Danny grasped his limp hand and shook it. The man's embracing smile graced a sunken, ashen face. Folds of skin hung from his wasted frame; a familiar sight to Danny who'd seen much of it in the course of visits to the cancer treatment center. The disease consumed a person from the inside out—rotted and hollowed-out their bodies, leaving only the stale, thin air of life to leak out of the shell at the very end.

"Everett Monteith here. Happy to meet you. Glad for the company," he said, voice raspy.

"Pleased to make your acquaintance. I'm Danny Burchard."

"Welcome to the family," Everett said.

"I beg your pardon?"

Everett smiled. "Well—we're related, I'm sure."

Was this man crazy?

Everett laughed and his face expanded with delight. "Get it? You and me. We both have Mister Big C mucking about in our bodies, don't we?"

Danny grinned. "Yeah—you too?"

"And everyone else in here. One big, happy family that's dying of cancer."

Danny marvelled at his roommate's dark humour. Most people

didn't realize that cancer patients *wanted* to talk about their troubles. This man's attitude and geniality was refreshing, in a morbid sort of way.

"Not upsetting you am I?" Everett said. "Find it helps to laugh. They gave me six months to live six months ago. It's a bummer. Been bed ridden ever since I got here. Held out as long as I could at home, but it became too much for my wife. How about you?"

"Told me I had six months, five months ago," Danny said.

Everett's eyebrows jumped. "Wow. They matched us up like a dating service. We're going to die at the same time. Now that's compatibility."

They both laughed. Danny hadn't done much of that lately. He liked this man and felt good about his decision to share a room.

"You play cribbage, Dan?"

"Yes."

Everett's hand thumped the side rail of his bed. "Wonderful. I've been looking for a partner. Maybe we can play sometime. Be forewarned though. I'm very competitive."

Over the next two weeks, Danny brought Everett books and magazines from the library, and played cribbage with him after lunch. Everett was a shrewd player and seemed to get a good hand most of the time.

"There's twenty-four in my hand and ten in the crib. You didn't get to sixty. That's a skunk," Everett said, in triumph one afternoon.

Danny shrugged. *Cards are only the luck of the draw, anyway.* "You killed me that time," he said.

"No, I didn't. Mister Big C is doing that, but he's not finished yet," said Everett.

Danny laughed. "With your luck, you should buy lottery tickets."

"Don't have the time to spend a big lottery win."

"Don't get too smug. I'll get even with you tomorrow," Danny said.

Everett smiled. "I told you I was hard to beat. Do your worst."

"You're a good guy, Everett. Wish I had met you before now."

"Me too, Dan. Don't get morbid on me now. We'll still have many fun times."

Elaine Monteith, Everett's wife, came to visit every other morning with home-baked treats, special meals, and news. A kind, regal-looking woman with a patrician bearing, wearing expensive jewellery, she soon included Danny in the culinary offerings. The food was delicious and stimulated his appetite. The warmth and companionship of people was a welcome change from the isolation of his small apartment relieved only by short visits from Meals on Wheels and Celine, the home nurse who didn't say much. The medication kept his pain at bay, as promised.

Watching Elaine's loving concern for her husband, Danny thought of his own short-lived marriage so long ago. He didn't want children. She did and called him selfish. They were incompatible and fought about small things all the time. There were a few girlfriends, but they all wanted commitment and none were ever good enough for a life partner. There would be no close relative to comfort him in his last days.

Danny was curious about his roommate. One day after cribbage he asked, "What did you work at before retiring, Everett?"

"I was in banking."

"A bank manager?"

"No, an investment banker."

"What's that?"

"My job was to create funds for the bank."

"How did you do that?"

"Mostly by selling stock and floating venture capital."

"I heard those venture capitalists were sharks."

"Well, we're more interested in cash than blood, although money is the lifeblood of financial markets. We loaned to start-up and young businesses in exchange for partial ownership of the company and a share of the profits."

"Sounds like an important job," Danny said. *This man had a career.*

Everett nodded. "Paid very well, but there's a great deal of responsibility. You need a master's degree in finance or business."

Danny remembered leaving school after grade ten. "You need an education to get anywhere in this world," his father had said. Danny considered that anything his parents suggested was stupid.

"How about you Dan? What did you work at?"

"I operated machines in a factory that made hardware. You know—metal hinges, brackets, connectors. It didn't pay much."

"Interesting. All jobs are important. Things need to be held together in this world. You live here in the city?"

"Yeah. Had a one-bedroom apartment in the west end. You?"

"We live north of the city on a lake-front property…" Everett hesitated and his smile dropped. "At least my wife Elaine does, now."

"Sounds nice," Danny said. A home of his own was always out of reach.

"It's a five-bedroom home on three acres with a boathouse. Incredible sunsets. The grandchildren love to visit. Before I got sick, we spent winters at our place in Arizona."

Danny walked over to the window and looked out. *Wonder what having children would have been like.*

"You married, Dan? Any children? Family?"

"Divorced a long time ago. No kids. No siblings. Folks are dead." Danny remembered his mother's last years. Rose Hospice reminded him of her nursing home. She always begged him to visit her more often. He should have.

"You like to travel, Dan?"

"I was saving up to take a trip to England when I retired," Danny said. "Always wanted to see Westminster Abbey and Buckingham Palace."

Danny looked at the sky. The dull panorama of his life compared to Everett's flashed through his mind like flipped pages of a magazine. He thought about not finishing high school, the menial jobs, a failed marriage, doing nothing extravagant or adventurous. Each segment seemed an ugly poster of mediocrity and failure compared to his roommate's full, prosperous existence filled with family, possessions and wonderful experiences.

Danny sighed. "It's too late for that now."

Everett smiled. "We travelled through Europe every year. I wanted to buy a place there before…"

His face flattened.

"You should see if the library has some travel books you might enjoy reading, Dan."

"Yeah, maybe some time."

Danny looked back at Everett and saw his face twist. "You in pain, Everett?"

"No, I'm okay."

Danny caught his own reflection in the glass. The disease had aged him. At that moment the sad realization settled on him—what he had made of his life and what he'd become as a person. He'd always been able to ignore the pricking of his conscience before, but now....

I'm not only ugly outside, but inside too. I lived a self-absorbed, narrow life, existing only for the moment. My parents begged me to go to college, but studying was too much effort. I could have worked at my marriage. She was a good woman. All she wanted was a family, but to me children were a nuisance. I was too good to share my life with anyone after that. If I'd taken courses to improve myself, I would have had a better job and been able to afford more of life's experiences. I had few real friends and cared little for others. Now it's too late.

The pangs of regret were like swallowing broken glass.

"What do you see out there, Danny?" Everett said. "From where I'm lying over here, all I can see is a band of blue sky."

Danny looked at him.

The poor guy can't even get up to look out the window. Aside from the short visits from his wife he has nothing left.

"I see a small lake surrounded by manicured green space with trees and bushes. It's beautiful."

"Are there flowers?" Everett said.

"Oh yes. Beds of gorgeous blossoms—all kinds and colours."

"What else?"

"Mothers with small children are in the park playground today."

"I remember when our boys were kids. They loved the park," said Everett.

"A father is floating a boat on the water with his son."

"I built model airplanes with my sons," Everett said.

"Look at that golden retriever fetching a ball. Boy, he sure can run."

"We had a Great Dane named Sultan," Everett said. "I loved that dog."

The next morning Elaine Monteith arrived with home-made Chelsea buns and a thermos of hot lemon-ginger herbal tea. She laid out a small table and two chairs beside Everett's bed. While eating and drinking, they talked about books and the upcoming municipal election.

"Ah, that tastes good." Everett said.

"Delicious. Thank you Mrs. Monteith," said Danny. He rose and walked to the window. She followed to stand beside him and look out.

"What's out there today," said Everett.

Danny looked at Elaine and raised a forefinger to his lips without Everett seeing.

"The grass is such a bright green in this early morning light," Danny said.

It's a dirty, black asphalt parking lot with potholes.

"Lots of pine trees. I'll bet they smell good," said Danny.

All you can see is that brick factory wall.

"We used to cut our own tree at Christmas," Everett said.

"The wind is blowing through the trees moving the branches like dancers, rippling the water on the lake and raising castles of turreted clouds high in the air," said Danny.

Dust, newspaper and discarded plastic bags are blowing around.

"Any birds?" Everett asked.

"I think I see an eagle up in the sky," said Danny.

There's only scruffy, grey pigeons perched on the edge of the factory roof. They look tired and defeated. The sign on the building says NICHOLSON MACHINERY COMPANY.

"What was the sunrise like this morning?" said Everett,

"Beautiful tones of yellow and red-gold on the horizon and a blue sky powdered with pink-tinged white clouds," said Danny.

The dull sky rests on top of that ugly factory building like icing on a decrepit cake. Beyond the building spreads the dark shingled roofs, chimneys, and grey, rectangular apartment buildings in the old section of the city. The smog made the morning sunrise appear like an incandescent light bulb obscured by a dirty lace curtain.

"Any people?"

"Two joggers and a woman with a pram."

Two winos sucking on a bottle of goof in a doorway.

"Sounds like a wonderful day," Everett said. "Beautiful world. I'm glad I could see it through your eyes, Danny, and take the memories with me."

"Real keeper of a day," said Danny.

He looked at Elaine. She glanced at her husband then turned to Danny with a smile. Her mild, green eyes were moist and her lips mouthed the words, "Thank you."

Danny nodded and smiled.

Danny took Everett's advice and read all the travel books from the library. Imagination was a wonderful thing. He'd never see those places but felt like he'd been there.

"Think of all the money you've saved on airfare and hotel rooms," Everett joked.

"Why don't we read some other books together?" he told Everett. "I'd like that."

Danny read *The Seven Story Mountain* by Thomas Merton, *The Lessons of History* by Will Durant and *The First And The Last* by Adolph Galland to his friend.

Danny could see his friend gradually getting weaker and felt the coldness in his own body creep deeper into his core with each passing day. Everett was very weak now, but resigned and at peace with himself.

"Yesterdays are gone forever, Dan. I've got no regrets. They're useless anyway, like trying to make footprints in a puddle of water."

Danny nodded. *Yes, it was true. For better or worse, his life had been lived. There was only so much sand in the hourglass. Not a single grain could be drawn back up. The only thing that mattered now was being as good a person as he could be for what time remained to him.*

Everett's joke, when they first met, about being well-matched was prophetic. Danny was bed-ridden now. Everett slept most of the day, almost comatose, oblivious to events around him. Danny woke up early, but slept after lunch, a book usually slipping from his hands as weakness and exhaustion overtook him. Bedtime came soon after dinner. He could feel time eroding him—the disease dismantling his body cell by cell like a building being taken apart brick by brick. His bones, covered by thin, blue-veined flesh felt like brittle sticks in a burlap bag. His body, the extremities cold and numb, felt hollow and used up—life seeping from it like water from a leaky tub.

An envelope came in the mail from Elaine Monteith: a thank you card with a bookmark. Danny set the envelope on his night table.

In the morning, the Filipino nurse came and looked in at Everett. She pulled a stethoscope from her pocket, applied it to his chest and then pulled a curtain around his bed. Cold snakes of dread slithered up Danny. His friend was gone.

Tears clouded his eyes and ran down his cheeks, dampening his pillow. He was truly alone now. It bothered him that he didn't take the opportunity to say goodbye to Everett. How do you part life with somebody? Do you just say, "It was nice knowing you?" No words would have seemed sufficient.

He smiled at the thought. Everett, always joking, might have said precisely that, adding the words, "Good luck" as if there was some future enterprise to be undertaken out there in the void.

Danny opened the thank you card. It read:

Danny:
Thank you for your kindness and friendship to my husband. Everett enjoyed your companionship and the accounts of events in the outside world you related to him each morning. It doesn't matter that their reality was different from what you described. The images stirred his imagination, raised his spirits, and wiped away, at least temporarily, the sour reality of his sickness, debility, and impending death. It meant a lot to him, and to me, in his last days. God bless you.
Elaine

He picked up the bookmark. A verse was inscribed on it.

As a tree sheds leaves to fertilize the earth for new life to come,
Our lives, if well-lived, spread love to feed the souls that retain a part of us.

11. VALLEY OF LOST YESTERDAYS

Larry always wondered what became of Adam. Every time he stood on the balcony of his condominium apartment overlooking the Don Valley he thought about the man he met so many years ago, when he was a boy. He never imagined that thirty years later he would gaze down from the twelfth floor of a tall building perched on the edge of the valley and have a view of the rise of land where they had their encounter. The circle of life was a cliché, and although often true, the place of his childhood adventure looked very different now.

A few years after that memorable day, they carved great gashes out of the Don Valley and laid wide, black asphalt roads for the expressway. Farther north of the Prince Edward Viaduct, huge apartment buildings sprouted like thick, ugly grey weeds on the plateaus bordering the urban sprawl of Don Mills. The roar of traffic and din of honking horns replaced the harmonious songs of birds.

There was no trace of the campsite Adam had occupied.

On a steamy, August day in 1955, Larry and his friends Charlie and Frank climbed the west hillside of the Don Valley, enjoying the shade provided by large trees covering the green slopes; their trunks soaring to the sky; the foliage of the branches joining in a continuous canopy. Wildflowers mottled the distant hillsides in a quilters-array of vivid colours. A narrow trail wound its way through tall bushes.

Birds of all types and colours darted through the maples, chirping and singing, their voices blending in musical counterpoint, unlike the silent gray pigeons and scruffy brown sparrows pecking at dirty scraps on the grimy city streets where they lived.

Squirrels scratched on bark as they propelled themselves up thick tree trunks. A large brown rabbit hopped away, crunching dry leaves and twigs as he went.

Houses lining Broadview Avenue in the distance and cars gliding silently in slow motion reminded Larry that the valley was only a thin green strip winding through the City Of Toronto, like a bright ribbon wrapping a grey package. The black iron-supporting grid work of the

Prince Edward Viaduct to the north, erected on massive piers, seemed like fingers clawing at the valley's belly. The city was slowly swallowing the verdant gorge like an animal devouring prey. Did his friends feel the same way?

Walking to the river's edge, he gazed into the stagnant, muddy brown water. Larry's father said they used to catch salmon in the river years ago. It must have been such a different place back then.

Ducks waddled off the far bank into the reeds bordering the water's edge. Flocks of birds flew south towards the lake. Hawks circled in the air above them. A large fowl with multicolour markings on its neck and a long tail burst out of the bushes and skittered away. "Wow. What kind of bird is that?" Charlie said.

Frank skipped a stone across the surface of the water, its journey terminating in the murky liquid with a plunking sound. "We should have brought our bathing suits," he said.

Larry looked at the sluggish water. An unpleasant smell drifted into his nostrils. Imagine swallowing any of it. He wondered if any life existed below its surface.

"Floating on a raft would be better, guys," he said. They would need a lot of boards and nails plus a hammer to make one.

"We should have brought bows and arrows," Charlie said.

Larry pulled down a sapling and released it. The trio watched the trunk spring back, leaves making a loud, swishing sound.

"We could bring a knife and some string to make our own," he said.

Charlie motioned with his arm. "Let's walk up past the Bloor Street Bridge." That was his name for it, but Larry's mom explained that its real name, The Prince Edward Viaduct, came from the King's son who visited the city many years ago.

They walked north to the viaduct, past wetlands filled with rushes and fluttering birds.

Standing on a slight rise below the intricate steel framework and concrete piers, Larry imagined they must look like ants to anyone on top.

Frank stretched his neck back. "Be fun to climb that."

Larry shivered. He didn't like heights.

"Wow," Charlie said, as he squinted at the green vista of the valley spread out in front of them, the river winding through it like a brown snake. "It goes on forever."

Frank gestured north. "Let's walk farther."

After they took a few steps, Charlie pointed at a small rise to the west. "Look at that."

Just visible through the bushes and trees, Larry could see fabric moving in the wind.

Frank shaded his eyes from the sun. "What the heck's that? Flags?"

"Might be a gang's camp," said Larry. "We'd better stay away."

"We'll sneak up on it and take a look," said Frank. "Don't be such a chicken."

Items of clothing hung on a line strung between two trees—a red plaid shirt, pair of jeans, boxer shorts and socks. Two small, grey tents were complemented by a lean-to shelter of boards and tarpaulins. A pot dangled from a metal rod suspended over a circular firepit ringed with stones. Around it stood three old, worn, chrome and vinyl kitchen chairs.

"Looks like a campsite," Charlie said.

There was no sign of anyone.

"Stay here," Frank said. He crept out of the bushes, walked in, looked into the shelters and then beckoned to Charlie and Larry.

Frank squatted and stuck his fingers in the ashes.

"Cold."

He looked into the pot over the fire pit and winced. "What's this shit?"

Near the tents sat a pile of rubbish: empty soup, spam, and pork and bean cans; rum, whisky and beer bottles; worn out tennis shoes, bread wrappers and some old clothes.

Charlie pushed open the flap of a tent. "Let's see what's inside." He stuck his head in, and then pulled back. "Whooph—stinks in here."

They found an old, filthy mattress, soiled blankets, and a backpack. Frank lifted one blanket up with a stick. "Probably filled with cooties," he said, holding it far away from his body and screwing up his face.

The lean-to contained a soiled sleeping bag and small suitcase. An orange crate serving as a shelf held canned foodstuffs, plastic plates, a knife, fork, and a box of tea bags. A kettle and large, corked soda bottles filled with water sat beside the crate.

Frank picked up one of the cans, sneering, "Campbell's vegetable soup. I hate this stuff."

Larry's gut tightened. "I don't think we should touch anything Frank."

"It's just a pile of fuckin' junk," Frank said, throwing the can to the ground.

Charlie grinned and laughed. "Let's smash all this fuckin' shit up."

Larry's body tensed and threads of fear crawled across his chest.

Frank and Charlie tore down the tents after throwing all the items outside.

Larry's heart pounded. *This stuff belongs to someone. What if they come back now?* "Guys—what are you doing?"

"Having some fun. Whaddya think?" said Charlie as he picked up the kettle by the handle and hurled it at a tree.

Frank kicked the pot down from the fire pit, emptied the bottles of water in the dirt and whooped as he flung cans of food into the bushes where they landed with thumps, raising streams of dust.

"Wahoo! Good bye tastes-like-shit soup."

After smashing an empty soda bottle on a rock, Charlie opened the small suitcase, turned it over and shook out socks, underwear, toothpaste, a toothbrush, a straight razor and some photographs. He picked up the razor, flipped it open and touched the edge of the blade with his finger. The sun glinted off the bright metal.

"Sharp as hell. Neat. We can cut things with this." He stuffed it into his pocket.

"Charlie you should put that back," Larry said. He looked around, perspiration running downs his cheeks, sweat-soaked T-shirt sticking to his chest. They continued to ignore him, kicking items around and raising clouds of grey dust.

Frank ripped down the clothesline, stomped on the clothes, and kicked the orange crate to pieces.

Charlie jumped on the empty suitcase, crunching it like a quart berry box. Larry looked all around. The sickening orgy of destruction frightened him.

Charlie and Frank laughed like hyenas while wiping their shoes on the clothes lying on the ground. "Always polite to wipe your feet when ya come into someone's place, eh," said Frank. Charlie guffawed.

"Hey! You!" a voice rang out.

A spike of terror ripped through Larry. He turned around to see a strange-looking man running toward them.

"Holy shit." Charlie dropped the underwear he was twirling around on a stick.

He and Frank took off running. Larry followed, but his companions drew well ahead of him, disappearing into the underbrush.

Larry ran as fast as his legs would take him, tripping, getting back up and dodging trees and bushes. His chest heaved and hurt. He raced frantically through tall grass, avoiding branches and rocks, his breathing a rasping noise in his throat. He heard the sound of heavy feet behind him. He glanced back. The large figure was gaining, the face stern and determined. He tried to run faster. His throat hurt and lungs felt ready to burst. His entire body screamed with pain; his mind frantic with fear.

He stumbled and tripped, scraping his leg and knee.

A strong hand pulled him up by the scruff of his T-shirt. Larry tensed for the beating which would likely follow.

"You should know better than to try and outrun an Indian," a voice behind him said.

Larry screamed. Tears blinded him. The man held his arm in a vice-like grip above the elbow and shook him. The pain was intense—Larry thought the bone would break.

"Shut up. No one can hear you down here," the man said.

Larry dug his feet into the ground and tried with all his might to pull away as the man dragged him towards the campsite, but it just made his arm hurt more. Sweat and dust covered his body and he choked for air. Blood oozed from the scratches and scrapes on his leg and arm and the sweat and dirt running into them made the abrasions sting. His leg muscles throbbed.

Larry thought of his home and mother. She was right about insisting he never come here. Terrible people lived in this valley and one had caught him. Why hadn't he listened?

"No—no—no," he pleaded, holding up his hand to ward off blows he was sure would come. This man would do terrible things to him. He remembered seeing Indians scalp and torture white men in the movies by making them run through a gauntlet of braves armed with clubs and tomahawks. Thoughts collided in his head like a crowd of boys exiting a schoolhouse door at the end of class. "No—

please—I'm sorry—I didn't do anything—my friends did it," he screamed through tears blurring his vision.

"Bullshit. I caught you and you're coming with me," the man said.

Larry shrieked louder. Surely someone would hear him?

The man stopped and pulled him up, his brown face inches away; dark eyes shining; discoloured, decayed teeth visible in a twisted mouth; breath sharp and foul. Was this the last face he would see on this earth?

"Be quiet, kid. You did a man's dirty work and you'll face a man's consequences."

Larry kept screaming. It would be the end of him, now.

"Shut up." The man shook him and the force made it feel like Larry's brain was rattling inside his skull, his consciousness drifting into a dark abyss.

"I'm not going to hurt you," the man said. The spittle gathering at the corners of his mouth made him look ferocious. He loosened his tight grip on Larry's arm, but the pain between his shoulder and elbow persisted.

Larry swallowed, sniffled and looked up at the man through blurred, water-filled eyes. Salty tears dribbled off his chin and snot ran into his mouth. He wiped a grimy hand across his mouth and nose, drawing a wet streak through the dust on the back of his hand.

The man's intense, penetrating eyes shone contrasted against his dark complexion. Larry had never seen a real Indian before. The man didn't look that old, but his thin face displayed deep pockmarks. Red threads ran through the whites of his eyes surrounding black pupils and his nose sat bulbous and veined on his face. Jet-black hair tied in a ponytail bore grey streaks around his temples. Scabs and odd-looking tattoos decorated his arms.

He raised his hand and pointed. "Walk back to the camp. I'll be right behind you so don't bother trying to run away."

Larry started walking but kept glancing back and sniffling. What torments awaited him there?

"Go on. Keep walking."

"What are you going to do to me?" Larry said, his mouth quivering.

"I'm not going to hurt you—promise."

Larry didn't believe him. His body shivered in spite of the heat. They were in the middle of nowhere with no one else around. This man could do anything to him and no one would ever know. He thought of his mother. She'd never find out what happened to him and he now understood why she'd ordered him never to come here. Why didn't he listen? He thought of a recent article in the newspaper about a girl in Scarborough who had disappeared without a trace. The same thing would happen to him—an unmarked grave in this valley.

They arrived at the campsite. The man put his hands on his hips surveying the broken, scattered items, and then looked down at Larry.

"Is this how your parents raised you? Didn't they teach you better? Why did you and your friends do this? I didn't do anything to you."

"It wasn't me. I didn't want to. They did it."

"Why should I believe you? You ran away. If you did nothing wrong, why did you run? Why didn't you tell your friends to stop?"

"I told them not to do it. I ran because I was scared."

"Words are easy, kid, but deeds tell the real truth. Only people who've done wrong and cowards run away."

Larry looked down at the ground. Charlie and Frank were his friends. He should have done more to make them stop.

The man pointed at the crushed suitcase. "Okay—now you're going to help make things right here. Go get that."

Larry picked up the flattened suitcase and brought it over. The man punched out the crumpled sides with his fist, but it was still a mess. Then he knelt, put the spilled items back in, gently picked up the black and white photographs and brushed the dirt off. After wiping one across his shirt he held it out to Larry.

"My mother and sister," he said, in a soft voice.

The two women in the photo wore traditional native dress and long braids. The older one had a glum expression, but the face of the young, attractive girl on the right had a slight smile. They wore decorative headbands and moccasins. Tall trees, a calm lake, and a birch bark canoe appeared in the background.

He pointed to the young girl. "My sister. She died of TB." He laid the photos in the suitcase and closed the lid. Larry sensed the sadness in his voice. Only a clasp on one side of the small suitcase secured the top. The other twisted corner displayed a large gap.

He pointed to the bushes. "Your buddy threw my cans of food

over there. Go get them."

Larry walked into the bushes just to the north of the site. The man didn't follow, which surprised him.

Is he testing me to see if I'll try to run?"

Now was his chance. Doubling back would be necessary to go south toward home. Going east or west were options, but a steep hill was on one side of the valley and the river separated him from the other side. Whichever way he tried to go, the man would easily catch him again and be even angrier. What should he do?

The man glanced in his direction. "Hurry. We have a lot of cleaning up to do here."

Larry's instinct told him that if the man was going to hurt him he would have done so by now. Fear was displaced by the tide of guilt which swept over him and he felt an obligation to help put things back the way they were. He picked up three cans lying in tall grass and returned to the camp site, holding them out.

"I only found these. I'm sorry—one is dented."

The man hefted the damaged can in one hand while turning it to view the label.

"Wasn't crazy about that soup anyway," he said, smiling.

He showed Larry how to re-pitch the tents and re-assemble the lean-to. They gathered the other scattered items, shook out the sleeping bags and blankets, and then replaced them in the shelters.

"Tie that clothesline back up," he said.

Larry re-tied the cord to the trees, picked up the clothes, shook out the dirt, and then draped the soiled items over the line. A white T-shirt was imprinted with the black impression of the sole of a shoe.

The man shook his head. "Billy and Roscoe ain't gonna be very happy coming back to the mess you guys made."

Larry looked around. *Were his friends Indians too? Would they arrive soon?*

The man picked up a piece of the orange crate lying in a mess of splintered kindling and dropped it. "Have to find another box. This one's only good for startin' the fire with now."

Remorse gnawing at him, Larry avoided making eye contact.

"What's your name kid?"

Larry looked up. The stranger was smiling.

"Larry."

"I'm Adam," he said, extending a hand with ragged, black

fingernails. Larry shook it.

The skin of Adam's palm was rough, like a burlap sack. He picked up one of the empty water bottles and tipped it. A few drops fell to the ground, making tiny, dark circles in the dust. He grinned. "Just have to get some beer now, I guess."

He picked up the kettle, righted the chairs, sat down in one, and gestured at another. "Take a load off your feet, Larry."

The torn, soiled, vinyl-covered chair rocked on the uneven ground. It felt odd sitting in a chrome kitchen chair, outside, in the middle of the Don Valley looking up at the blazing sun and clear, blue sky. Larry's mother had the same chairs in her kitchen. Hard to believe that people lived out here in the open and not in a house. Wouldn't they be cold in the winter?

"Can't offer you nothin'," Adam said. "You guys spilled all the water and I ain't got any beer." He gave a tobacco-stained smile. "You're too young for that, anyway, aren't ya."

"Yeah," Larry said. Charlie stole a bottle of beer from his father once and let him have a sip. It tasted terrible, but someone said that if you kept trying it, you'd get used to the taste and eventually would like it. Larry doubted that, but he wanted to try smoking.

"How old are you Larry?"

"Eleven."

"Where do you live?"

"On Gerrard Street."

"In a house?"

"Yeah."

"Is it a nice one?"

"It's okay."

"You have your own room?"

"Uh huh." Larry was afraid Adam would ask his address, but he didn't.

"You're lucky. I didn't have my own room as a kid. Six of us lived in one small house."

Larry looked at the campsite. "Are you a hobo, Adam?" His dad had said there were many of them travelling around after the big depression in 1929, but this was 1955 and that depression was long past. When Larry asked what a depression was, his father replied, "It's when people don't have jobs or money."

Adam threw his head back and laughed. "That's as good a title as any, I suppose. Yeah, this is my home. It ain't much, but it's all I have. It was better before you and your gang busted it all up."

Larry felt a flush of shame rise in his cheeks. His mother would be very angry if she knew what they'd done.

"I'm sorry—I really am. I told them it wasn't right, but they wouldn't listen to me. I swear it."

Adam looked at him, paused, pressed his lips together and nodded twice. "Y'know—I think you *are* sorry. I'm an Indian and we can tell when a man is lying."

That's scary. How can he tell? Larry made up his mind not to lie. He remembered what a character in a western movie had said and repeated it: "You mean when a man's speaking with a forked tongue?"

Adam closed his eyes, laughed and slapped his thigh. A puff of dust rose from his trousers. "You've watched too many movies kid. We don't say that. It's Hollywood white man's talk."

The movies always portrayed Indians as cruel, vicious enemies to be fought and killed. This man seemed ordinary aside from the fact that he looked different and lived outdoors in the Don Valley. "I never met an Indian person before," Larry said.

"Am I what you thought one would be?"

"Uh… no."

"You expected feathers, tomahawks and moccasins I guess—like the movies, eh?"

"Yeah, sort of."

Adam smiled. "I should'a given war whoops when I chased you down."

Larry grinned.

"Too bad I lost my scalping knife."

Larry stopped smiling. *Was he joking about that?*

"We used to be different before your ancestors came and changed us—took our land, and way of life."

There was a trace of bitterness in Adam's voice and Larry felt heavy inside. Was what he said true? Had other people done bad things to Indians?

"How long have you lived here Adam?"

"Too long." Adam pointed up towards Bloor Street. "Better than the street up there though—too crowded. I'm a Cree from Chapleau."

"What're those things?"

"Cree's my tribe. There's many different Indian tribes, like there's many different nationalities of white people. Chapleau is a place way up north. The air's good there. Lots of fish and game. You can live off the land if you want to. This city stinks."

Larry remembered his vacation at Carrying Place near Trenton. The air was fresh and there were lots of fish in the bay. "Sounds neat. I'd like to go there someday."

Adam smiled. "Yeah? Maybe we can go together."

Larry wasn't sure about living outside with Adam. "I'd have to ask my mother."

"Sure—I get it, kid. What grade you in?"

"Six."

"You like school."

"It's okay." Larry hated school. It was mid-August. That meant classes would be starting again in September right after the Canadian National Exhibition was over.

"Stay in school kid. Get an education. I never went to school. They wanted to take me and my sister away to a residential school, but my old man wouldn't have it. He took us into the bush and we lived by hunting and fishing. The stupid government jerks couldn't find us. I learned to survive in the wilderness, but not to read or write properly."

Larry didn't know what Adam meant by a residential school and was surprised that there were kids who never had to attend school.

"Indian people didn't have reading and writing before you white people came. Did you know that?"

"No, I didn't."

"And do you know why they called us Indians?"

"No."

Adam sneered. "Because the early white explorers were so stupid, that when they came here they thought it was the country of India on the other side of the goddam world so they called us Indians. There are real Indians living in India, but we aren't them."

"I didn't know that," Larry said.

"I joined the army in 1939 when the war started. They didn't care that I couldn't read or write worth a damn. I was healthy and a crack shot—exactly what they needed. I signed up at twenty-one. Times were tough and it was an opportunity to see the world, get fed and have some adventure. Just had to make a mark on their paper, was all."

"You were in the war?"

"Overseas for six years—a sniper."

"You killed guys with a rifle?"

"Yeah. Lots o' them. The army loved Indians for sniping—our special talent, y'know. Need good eyes for that. The drink's made me sick now, but my eyes are still good."

"What was it like?"

"To shoot someone, y'mean?"

"Yeah."

"It was easy. You plug them from a distance so you don't see their faces up close."

"How'd you feel after doin' it?"

"Funny at first, but you get used to it. Soon it's not like you're shootin' real men anymore, just greenish-gray lumps like walking sacks of potatoes. After a while I didn't feel nothin'. Killin' was my job and I was good at it."

Adam raised his arms like he was holding a rifle, moved in an arc and stopped.

"You hold real still, see—aim for the center of their chest and squeeze the trigger slowly." He curled his index finger over an imaginary trigger. "Bang."

Lowering his hands, he said, "It's not dramatic dyin' like in the movies. They just stop in their tracks and crumple to the ground dead."

"Jeez," Larry said. He and his friends played at being soldiers, but he couldn't imagine killing anyone for real.

"Sometimes I'd aim for their heads just for fun, but ya gotta be right on to do that, 'specially if they have a helmet on. Most times I could hit them right in the center of the forehead."

Larry swallowed and grimaced at the thought of being shot in the head. "Sounds easy bein' a sniper."

"The shooting part was. The harder part was the other guys in my troop that looked down on me at first because I was an Indian. They called me injun and squaw soldier."

"What did you do?"

Adam curled his right hand into a fist and smacked his palm.

"I earned their respect with my rifle against the enemy and my fists against them in camp. I beat the shit out of every guy that said a jackassin' word to me, one by one. Soon they learned I was as tough as they were and as good a soldier."

Pride flashed in Adam's dark eyes and a smile raised his cheeks.

"After the war, the government dropped me in Halifax and I just drifted here."

"Why didn't you go back home to that Chapello place?"

"Hard to explain. Folks were dead and nothin' seemed important anymore. Somethin' inside bothered me, like a tree havin' a beaver chewin' chips off it, but I didn't know what it was. Couldn't see it and couldn't fight it."

He lowered his head. "Tried to bury it with the drink. Still tryin'."

Larry knew his sister's husband, a war veteran, drank a lot. That was different though, wasn't it?

Larry looked at Adam and tried to swallow the lump in his throat. The man seemed tired and worn, like the act of existing had eroded him. The guilt at what he and his friends had done to Adam's camp and sorrow for what the man's life had turned out to be pricked at him. His family didn't have much money, but he thought of his mother's warm kitchen infused with the fragrant odour of cooking and his clean bedroom with fresh white sheets every week. Living outside without having a real home, proper food or a family was unimaginable and compared to Adam, he lived in luxury.

"They teach you about us Indians in school?"

"No."

Adam jabbed a forefinger at him. "I'm gonna tell ya about my people so ya know."

Larry nodded. "Okay."

"All you white people understand about us is from the movies and how we're shown as your enemies. That's a lotta crap. We were a nation the same as where your people came from. This was *our* home, which your people from across the ocean claimed to discover. The truth is that we welcomed you here. We believed the land was given to all people and you would share it with us in peace, but you tricked us, took it all for yourselves, killed us and made us prisoners in reserves. Our lives you didn't take with guns and starvation, you took with your diseases. We caught them and died like grass being flattened by the blowing wind."

"But you're not in a reserve now. You're free," Larry said.

"Not like you are. I've never been really free; never had the same rights and opportunities as you white people. The government made special laws for us. I don't feel like a Canadian. Real Canadians have rights and are treated with respect."

"I respect you."

"You didn't when you smashed up my camp. Would you go into a friend's house and do that?"

He was right. Larry looked down at the ground, the heat of shame rising up his neck and cheeks.

Adam pulled Larry's chin up with his sandpaper-rough fingers. "Look a man straight in the face when he's talking to you."

"Sorry."

Adam's eyes widened and his face twisted with anger. "Polak and German immigrants are more Canadian than I am. They screwed up Europe, and then came over here. The Germans were our goddam enemies, but our government let them into this country after the war. They didn't pass any special laws for them. They killed our soldiers, but had rights as soon as they got off the boat—more rights than I did. There ain't any reserves for Germans here. When I came back people spit at me and called me a dirty Indian, but they gave the krauts jobs and called them sir."

There was a boy from Germany in Larry's class at school. They made fun of his accent. "But you fought for Canada. You should have rights."

Adam laughed. "That's somethin' else. We'll bleed and die for you white people, but not for ourselves. You call us to fight in Europe and we go. We'll fight and spill our guts on the ground for the Korean chinks five years later, but not for our own women, children and culture your people have destroyed for three hundred years."

Fire glowed in Adam's eyes. Except for the movies, Larry had never thought much about Indians before. Was everything he said true? He'd ask his mother. She'd know.

Adams voice elevated. His face smouldered with a rage turned inward. "No one can give you your rights. You have to fight for them and take them. Otherwise, you don't deserve to have them." He closed his eyes for a moment. "You know what a cigar store Indian is, kid?"

"Yeah—an Indian statue carved out of wood. I saw one near Carrying Place outside a store."

"That's what we are now—wooden Indians—not real men anymore."

It was all confusing to Larry.

"I don't mean you any harm when I say it kid, but you and every other white person is my enemy. Think about that."

Larry tensed and drew back. "You want to fight us all?"

"It's too late for that now. We couldn't win then, and we can't now."

The world Adam described was upside-down—foreign and cruel. *Weren't we all the same in Canada; everyone equal, with the same rights and everything? That's what they said at school.*

"And think about how you busted up my stuff, but I forgave you and didn't hurt you. Indians are good people."

Larry sensed Adam's hurt and despair. A constriction like a ratcheting steel band tightened around his chest. He wanted to apologise for their spur of the moment destructive impulse; say that he wasn't a bad person, how it was just things they were smashing, not people's homes, possessions and lives; tell him how sorry he was for everything that happened to his people.

"I'm—,"

"Never mind, kid. You can go now." Adam waved his hand.

Larry tried again. "But I—"

"It's okay. Go back to your nice house and family."

Larry walked away, stopping at the edge of the campsite to wave goodbye. Adam smiled, waved back, and looked away.

Larry walked home. He'd tell his mother he got the scratches on his leg and knee when he fell down playing ball in the school yard. He'd be punished if she knew the truth.

For two days, he avoided the friends who accompanied him to the Don Valley. On the third, he encountered them as they came out of the corner variety store. They looked different to him somehow— meaner and uglier.

Charlie flashed a twisted grin. "Hey Lar. Where did you go after that hobo guy came after us?"

"I ran away, just like you guys did. Thanks for not waiting for me, assholes."

Frank came close. Larry tensed for the punch he thought was coming. Frank was bigger than he was, but Larry felt anger rise in him and was ready to fight back.

Frank's flat face lifted in a grin and he shrugged. "Hey—it was every man for himself, eh?"

"Friends don't abandon their buddies, Frankie."

"So what? You got away, didn't you?"

"Yeah." *Fuck you both. I'm not admittin' he caught me.*

"Stop bellyachin' about it then, willya."

"So where ya been lately?" Charlie said.

"Around."

"Wanna do something tomorrow?"

"No, I'm busy. Gotta go now."

Frank's voice followed him as he walked away. "Okay, be a prick then, asshole."

Larry couldn't get Adam out of his mind. Guilt still gnawed at him for what they'd done. Maybe he and Adam could be friends. How many kids had a real Indian person for a friend? Adam could teach him about how his people made bows and canoes and lived in the wilderness.

"Have you ever known any Indians," he said to his mother, at lunch.

"No. They're all a bunch of good-for-nothings. They won't work. All they want is the drink that makes them crazy. I saw them begging on the street when I lived in Saint Gabriel De Brandon, Quebec."

"When was that, Mom?"

"In nineteen thirty-four—during the depression."

"Dad said many people did that then. Were there white people like us begging there too?"

"Well, yes, there were some white people doing that, but all Indians are like that."

"Do the Indians have same rights as us?"

"Everyone has the same rights in Canada. It's a free country. They must have taught you that in school."

Larry was confused. Who to believe? Everything was mixed up.

Shafts of sunlight streamed through his bedroom window the following Saturday morning. The crisp, spotless bed sheets his mother had put on the previous day swished as his feet kicked them off. The smell of breakfast drifted up from the kitchen: Dad's coffee and the pancakes Mom made every Saturday.

He pulled out the box holding six dollars he'd saved bit by bit to buy plastic model airplane kits, and put the money in his pocket.

After breakfast, Larry walked back to Adam's campsite in the Don Valley.

Adam sat on one of the kitchen chairs eating from a brown paper bag. The neck of a green bottle poked out from the top of another bag at his feet. He wore a plaid shirt, jeans shiny with grime, and lace-less tennis shoes without socks. His ankles were ringed with dirt. He looked up and smiled as Larry approached.

"Hey Larry. Surprised to see you back so soon."

"Hi Adam."

Adam picked up the bag with the bottle, took a drink and wiped his mouth. "Nice of you to come visit me."

Larry smiled, pulled the six dollars from his pocket and extended his hand. "Came to give you this."

Adam laid down the bottle, took the money, looked at it, then back at Larry. His eyes hardened and face twisted into a sarcastic sneer.

"What's this? You a charity worker or somethin'?"

Larry stiffened. "I—"

"Didn't you learn anything the last time you were here?"

Larry was confused by Adam's anger. "I just came to—"

"You did wrong bustin' up my things and said you were sorry. I believed you and forgave you. All I wanted was your respect and friendship, not your money."

Larry felt his throat tighten and his face flush.

Adam crumpled the bills and tossed them on the ground. "You said you were sorry and helped put things back the way they were. We talked together in friendship, like men. A man's character and actions are his *real* currency, not paper money. My people lived without money. You white people gave us your money, and then took our land and lives with your diseases and hate. Your dollars were a curse."

Larry looked down. The edge of one bill fluttered in the light breeze. "I'm sorry. I didn't mean—"

"I hoped that you—just one white person in this world, might understand." Adams voice elevated. "But your mind is poisoned just like all the rest."

Larry averted his gaze.

Adam pointed at his chest. "Look at me. Look at where I live."

Larry looked up. Adams eyes seemed to penetrate deep into his soul.

He swept his arm back. "Look all around you, kid. This place where you came to play isn't the valley of yesterday. It's the piss-hole of now—the valley of *lost* yesterdays; polluted, stinking, shrunken and destroyed by your people. The animals are gone."

"I saw animals here," Larry said.

"You saw the wretched remains of what used to be—creatures struggling to exist, just like I am. Once there were deer and bear here. The water was sweet on the tongue. The animals were our brothers and when we took them for food and clothing we gave thanks to their spirits because we are all one in this world. There's no fish in that river now. The birds fly on air filled with poison. Before long everything will be gone."

Larry's throat felt as if it had a stone stuck in it. He wiped his eyes.

"You cryin' for me or this place?" Adam said.

Larry was sad for both and could hardly breathe.

Adam continued. "Soon they'll put roads here and I'll not even have this piece of ground to live on or the dignity to be what I am." He pointed up to the top of the east hill. "I'll have to live up there, on your city streets, choking on filth; an unwelcome stranger in your white people's world."

Adam's words stung Larry like windswept, cold sleet.

"Pick up your money and go kid. You ain't learned nothin'."

Larry collected the dusty bills, put them in his pocket and looked at Adam. His eyes were closed and he grimaced. He motioned Larry away.

"Leave. Now."

Larry looked back when he reached the edge of the campsite. Adam's upper body was bent over, holding the paper-wrapped green bottle in his hands.

Walking out of the valley towards home, he had much to think about.

The screeching tires of the never-ending bumper to bumper crunch of the Don Valley Parkway shook Larry out of his recollection. The vehicles were like metal canines pursuing females, their snouts pushing into the backsides of the ones preceding them. Much of the vegetation and many of the trees down there were gone now, the perfume of their foliage replaced by the stench of vehicle exhaust. In the distance, smoke from the factories near the lake draped over the mouth of the river like a shroud and on certain days, depending on the wind, the odours from the soap factory and abattoir to the south drifted in the air.

He glanced at the cup of coffee in his hand, cold now after his morning reverie. Time to join the parkway conga line of traffic for the trip downtown.

Stepping back inside and closing the patio door did not silence the cacophony of traffic, nor eradicate the foul odour arising from the putrid lake that was once the Valley.

12. WITNESSES

I had no idea that my husband Gregory wanted to murder me.

He gave no outward indication of his dissatisfaction with our marriage. I thought we were happy. After we married, I realized that he tended to be self-absorbed and lazy, but everyone has his faults. We had our disputes like all couples do, but I loved him and thought he loved me in return.

How long had the thought of killing me been on his mind? What were the reasons? Did you need only *one* to embark upon murdering someone?

Did I nag or criticize him too much? If I did, it was because I cared. Was it for money? He knew he'd get my insurance money and inherit everything. I wonder if he had a mistress.

When did he make the decision to do it?

The idea of committing murder didn't bother him. It seems conscience and scruples were not among his attributes. He was unconcerned that the penalty for murder in our state is death.

My killing must have been planned with care. Having been a lawyer, I know that committing the perfect murder requires consideration of a number of issues: when and how to do it, not leaving evidence, and having a solid alibi. Acting in emotion or haste can lead to mistakes—fatal ones.

If he hated me so much it must have taken considerable effort for him to subdue resentment and avoid arguments in order to appear the ideal, devoted, loving husband. He couldn't afford to attract suspicion by displaying rancour.

I can imagine him wrestling with the question of where to kill me. Doing it at home would be easy, but believable evidence of an accident, or intrusion by persons unknown would have to be contrived—a tricky thing to do.

He talked about taking a Mediterranean or Baltic cruise. Was he thinking about throwing me overboard during a midnight stroll on an isolated deck? He would realize I might scream and attract attention. Cruise ships account for all guests on embarking and disembarking so he'd have to report me missing. There'd be questions and without proof of my death, I couldn't be declared deceased until seven years had passed—too long for him to wait for the life insurance payout. He was always a somewhat impatient person.

What weapon to use? There were a number of choices. Guns would create too much noise and he'd have to purchase a firearm. The Record of Sale would attract suspicion.

Using a dagger was too unpredictable. Most victims don't die right away, especially if the knife-wielder is careless or inexperienced. He would have researched that. I wonder if poisoning occurred to him. I drank a glass of wine every evening and he could have mixed it with that. Gregory likely realized there would be an autopsy and the lethal compound would be discovered. He would be the natural suspect.

When I think about it, the method he settled on made sense.

*

I was surprised when he offered to drive me to and from the office on evenings I worked late. I was a partner in a litigation law firm and often worked almost to midnight on important cases. He wasn't inclined to be so considerate and attentive, but I welcomed the change in his behaviour and had no suspicion at that time.

"That's so nice of you Greg. I appreciate it, honey," I said. "You know how I hate driving in the city and at night."

Now I know that the trips were dry runs—an easy way for him to inspect the location: parking level three in the building on Market Street where I worked. At 11:20 p.m. when he picked me up, it was always deserted.

"I'll be late on Friday, darling. The McKenna versus Wright case goes to court the following Monday," I said to him, two days before.

"Okay dear, but you'll have to drive yourself," he said.

"Oh? Why?"

"I'm going out for dinner with the guys. It's a milestone birthday party."

I didn't question the change, whose birthday it was, or the location of the event. He was always annoyed when I inquired about his comings and goings.

*

Friday, August 12, 1966 was the perfect day for him to execute his plan. Everyone would be gone for the summer weekend except me—workaholic Sarah. My boss said he was recommending me for partnership in the firm.

"Anyone else working late?" Gregory said.

"No, the others hate to delay their weekends." I didn't suspect the ulterior motive for his question.

In retrospect, I realize how foolish I was to marry him. He swept me off my feet with his good looks and debonair manner, but only married me for my money. Even lawyers can be stupid and blind when it comes to romance.

My parents disliked him and urged me not to marry him. "Nothing but a gold-digger," my father remarked. I wonder if Gregory overheard Dad. Mom always acted cool and aloof towards him. Gregory disliked her. Did she sense something I didn't?

I was exhausted from work that evening.

The area was dark when I descended the elevator to Parking Level 3. The light near the elevator was out. Had he tampered with the bulb? It was quiet and empty. The place had a cold, damp smell, like a subterranean crypt.

On the way to the car I had to walk past an alcove in the wall. That's where he was hiding, ready to strike. I can imagine him listening for the sound of the elevator door opening and my heels clicking on the pavement; his body tense, mouth dry, holding the weapon in a gloved hand.

How long had he waited there? Did any needles of doubt or guilt prick at him? There are always unforeseen factors in schemes like that—things that can't be anticipated or controlled. What if I didn't come down alone? Would his brutal act be interrupted by another late-night driver? Suppose he encountered someone upon leaving? What if he left evidence behind? He must have analyzed the plan over and over, examining all possible contingencies. Nothing was foolproof. Police always suspect the husband.

I stopped to retrieve car keys from my purse. I can visualize him gritting his teeth, raising the weapon and holding his breath. As I came adjacent to the alcove I sensed his movement and turned but didn't see the blow to my head coming an instant later.

The experience was a brief moment of the most intense pain

imaginable, followed by bright lights and a sensation of levitation. I drifted above the scene, watching as he struck me two more times. My skull split open with a sickening crunch, reducing my head to a pulp of white bone, grey oozing brain, blood-soaked blond hair, and pink flesh.

It took a few moments for me to realize it was my own butchered, mortal body lying on the ground. I never imagined the end of life would be like it was: lightness and detachment from the physical world, but with an omniscient awareness. I was beyond any pain—the life driven from me, yet cognizant, feeling still alive, and floating above everything as an observer. It was like watching a panoramic scene from a movie.

I'm sure Gregory wondered if I had recognized him. I did. The twisted, murderous hatred on his face was unlike anything I'd ever seen. This was the man I loved and shared everything with; the person I committed my life to.

Why did you do this to me I screamed, but realized words uttered by the dead to the living remain unheard. I could not retaliate, merely watch.

He looked around, grabbed my blood-stained purse, ripped the expensive necklace from around the neck of my corpse and pulled a diamond bracelet from my wrist. Trying to avoid stepping in a pool of thick blood, he took what had been my most prized possession: a ring from the third finger of my left hand. He left my wedding band and diamond earrings.

*

I remembered the day we bought that ring. It was for our engagement and must have cost him all the money he had, and more. To him it was cynical, cool benevolence—an investment which would pay interest when I was dead.

"Pick the one you want," he said, smiling.

The display case in the jewellery store was filled with beautiful rings of all types but the uniqueness and beauty of that one captivated me; not a classic engagement ring, but one that drew me to it at once with its compelling exquisiteness; an attraction between us like the opposite poles of two magnets.

A large, central faceted stone set in a gold mounting gleamed with undulating shades of blue-green and magenta, depending upon how it was oriented to the light. Surrounding it was a circle of stones alternating in white diamonds and dark green emeralds. The most beautiful thing I ever saw.

"The central stone is Alexandrite," said the jeweler. "Quite rare and found only in Russia. It's named in honour of Czar Alexander II and has been called emerald by day, ruby by night from the shades of colour it emits from exposure to different light sources. This one was cut from a larger, ancient gemstone. Legend has it that the original stone belonged to a queen and has special mystical properties. It's quite unique."

I didn't believe that sales talk, then, and wanted it for its beauty but changed my mind when I slipped it on my finger. The fit was perfect without resizing. It seemed to grasp my finger with digits of its own and radiate a primordial energy up my arm and into my chest like the *vena amoris* the Romans used to refer to. A strange vision of a woman dressed in gold flashed through my mind and I felt an inexplicable kinship with her, whoever she was. The ring instantly became a part of me and an extraordinary surge of energy went direct to my heart. Now, I know that force was not the power of Gregory's love.

I had the inside of the band engraved with SR 1962—the initials of my name, Sarah Richmond and the year of our marriage.

Gregory looked at my splayed corpse on the walkway with a shoe hanging off one foot. He wiped the blood-stained black pipe on my skirt and watched a rivulet of my blood flow down a crack in the curb and soak into the black, greasy dirt.

I watched as he pushed my jewellery into his jacket pocket, put the pipe, gloves and my purse in a black bag, and look all around. The area was clear and quiet. He pulled a cap down on his head, glanced at my still corpse one last time and then walked to the stairs. I followed, unknown and unseen by him, drifting in the ether above his head.

He didn't run. Looking ordinary was a wise thing to do. People look suspicious when they run, even more so at night. The impulse must have been hard to resist, but he walked unhurried up the stairs, stopping once to glance back. The street was deserted. He proceeded east on Market Street, pulling the hat farther down on his head. As he removed car keys from his pocket my ring fell out and dropped to the ground, unnoticed by him. I hovered, looking at it.

Gregory's footsteps and form faded into the mist. I imagined he would dispose of the weapon, his blood-spattered clothes and my purse before going home to bed. In the morning he would report me missing and feign grief at being informed of my death—the devoted, caring husband act. Perhaps he would shed some contrived tears when they came to tell him I'd been robbed and murdered. Oh, they'd have questions, but he'd be a good actor.

I drifted over the street for days and nights watching my ring remain undetected by the busy eyes of the passers-by. It shone and beckoned to me, perhaps despairing its loss of my person but I, without substance now, could not reconnect it to me. Soon, dirt and debris partially obscured it.

As I coasted above, the rage about what had been done to me rose into silent screams of despair and anguish. The betrayal of my trust and love tormented me—my murder, tearing me from life, a desecration of a sacrosanct bond between husband and wife. Gregory had never loved me. He used me in his deceitful, evil design, planned, I believe, from early in our marriage. Others I loved might also suffer from his monstrous action. Would my father, with his weak heart die of shock and grief at the loss of his daughter? Would my mother become a shattered widow existing in a prison of bereaved loneliness for the remainder of her days?

I resolved that Gregory Richmond must be brought to account and punished. The scales must be re-balanced—loss for loss, justice against evil. As I was now without flesh or muscle, I needed allies to accomplish it. One, which was once united to me, lay on the ground below. With time, another would come to join us.

That time came—a city worker with *Dennis* stitched across his uniform. He pulled up to the curb and stepped down from his truck. He removed a bag of refuse from a street container and installed a new, empty one. Then he took a broom and dustpan from the back of the vehicle and started sweeping fragments of broken glass from an earlier accident, towards the curb. As he moved an empty, discarded cigarette package in the gutter with his broom, he uncovered my ring caked with grit.

Pick it up Dennis.

He glanced left and right, paused, then pocketed the ring. He deposited the contents of the dustpan in the sidewalk garbage container, returned to his truck and drove away. I followed.

On arriving home, Dennis rinsed my ring with warm water and cleaned dirt from its crevices with an old toothbrush. I suppose that from time to time he found lost items in the course of his work, but he seemed very pleased with finding my ring. He turned it over and over in his hand, admiring it.

"Hmm…eighteen carat gold band. Wonder if the stones are real?" he mumbled. "What does SR 1962 stamped inside the band mean?"

Soon you will know, Dennis.

He set my ring on his nightstand, had dinner, watched television, talked to his girlfriend Angela on the telephone and then went to bed. He fell asleep, and I entered his dream.

The elevator doors opened and I walked out. A sign near the door read LEVEL 3. Dennis followed me as I walked, looked at the back of my head with its blond, coiffed hair and watched my feet move one in front of the other. I stopped for a few moments to retrieve keys from my purse, and then continued, coming adjacent to a recess in the wall. As I turned to look into the alcove, a gloved arm bearing a blunt object struck me. Dennis saw my head split open and blood gush out. As I fell to the ground Gregory emerged from the recess to strike me, again and again. Dennis watched as Gregory took the jewellery from my body.

Next, in his dream, Dennis drifted up a stairwell and found himself standing alone on the shore of a red ocean. My corpse bobbed in the foam of blood-red waves and my hand moved to scratch the initials SR in the sand.

Dennis awoke, disturbed, and I gathered from his demeanor that his head throbbed with pain and his eyes burned from restless sleep. Sitting at the kitchen table holding a cup of hot, black coffee, his hand trembled. He tried steadying it, but liquid slopped over the rim, almost burning his fingers. His body appeared tense. He swallowed pills and rubbed his hands over his face.

Tell them Dennis. You've seen my murderer. He must be punished. Tell them what happened to me. Be my witness. Secure vengeance and justice for me.

He remained sitting.

Why are you not acting? Surely you don't think these horrific visions arose from the suspense novel you read before bed, or the spicy take-out chicken paprikash you consumed for dinner?

After showering, he picked up my ring from the nightstand and left the apartment.

I followed him to the store with the three-ball fixture suspended over its entrance—a pawn shop. He looked in the window filled with purple and red felt-lined trays holding rings, jewellery and watches.

Yes, Dennis. Those gold wedding bands and engagement rings testify to the transient nature of romantic love—each item someone's heartbreak and broken dream of forever after. This is why we are together, you and I. You will be my witness and bring me vengeance and justice. You will bring me peace.

A bell tinkled as the door opened. This place was filled with the castoffs of human existence: television sets, guitars, sports equipment, tools, and even a fancy leather saddle with high, shiny size ten riding boots. Musical instruments of all kinds dangled from the ceiling. A row of grandfather clocks stood with light reflecting off ornate gold-coloured dials and lyre pendulums.

The proprietor looked up as Dennis approached the expansive glass counter.

"Yes sir. Can I help you?" the man said. The sleeves of his white shirt were rolled up to the elbows. A faded, nondescript tattoo decorated one forearm. Alert, inquiring eyes looked out from a puffy face with bushy eyebrows; the balding head sporting a rim of steel-grey hair.

Dennis passed him my ring. "Can you tell me if this is of any value?" he said.

It is the most valuable thing in the world to me, Dennis.

"It's a very unusual and attractive piece. Where'd you get it?"
"Uh, it belonged to my mother. It's a family heirloom."

Why are you lying, Dennis? Tell him it belonged to me and what happened.

The proprietor glanced at my ring, then at Dennis. His head nodded and brow furrowed. He pulled down magnifying loupes over his eyeglasses and examined the ring, orienting it at different angles to catch the light from the overhead fluorescent fixtures. Next, he pulled out a testing device with probes connected to it. He turned a switch on the device and touched the large central stone with the probes. The needle on the tester swung across the face of the dial.

"The stones appear to be real, at least the large central one. If they are, the ring could be quite valuable," he said.

Dennis smiled.

"You're sure you received this from your mother?"

"Uh, yes. It's—an heirloom—quite old."

You know that's not true, Dennis.

The pawnbroker's lips pursed as he examined the ring.

"Hmm…old you say? The cut of the stones and design of the mount looks fairly modern. Did you want to borrow against it or sell it?"

"Not sure. Tell me what you'll give for it."

If you sell my ring it will only mean that I'd have a new ally; a different witness.

The pawnbroker laid the ring on the glass countertop and lifted the magnifiers from his eyes. "Give me a few minutes. I have to look up something in the back office. Have a seat. I'll be right back."

Dennis was able to see the pawnbroker through the small window in the door. The man was on the telephone—glancing to the outer limits of the shop as he spoke. Dennis snatched up my ring, rushed out of the store, crossed the street and went down into the subway, losing himself among the crush of bodies in the crowded subterranean space.

Later, I followed him into a jewellery store. Will he try to sell my ring here?

The young clerk at the counter smiled. "Yes, sir. How may I help you?"

"Will you please sell me a ring box, Miss?"

The girl laughed. "Just the box, sir? No ring to go in it?"

"I already have a nice ring for my girl—just need a box to put it in."

So you're not going to sell it. You're going to give it to your girlfriend.

"Let me guess. You're giving her your mother's ring? A family heirloom tradition thing, eh?"

Dennis shrugged. "Well, kind of."

"A lady will take a ring from a guy any way she can get it. Engagement?"

"Uh, no—just a gift. Giving it to her tonight."

She opened a drawer filled with black, felt boxes and pulled out one. "How's this?"

Dennis opened it, took my ring from his pocket and pushed it into the red velveteen slot. A perfect fit. The clerk craned her neck to see. Her eyes widened and she drew her breath in.

"Ohhhh…it's gorgeous. Your girlfriend is so lucky. It'll be a Friday evening she won't forget."

Dennis snapped the lid closed. "Thanks. How much for the box?"

She waved her hand. "Oh, no charge sir. We've got a ton of them. Keep us in mind when you need other jewellery. If she wants to sell that ring or trade it in, we can give her a great deal. Would you like me to clean it for you? We have a cleaner that does a great job."

"No, it's okay," Dennis said.

"If she wants to re-design it in a different setting we can do that too."

"I'll tell her."

She gestured toward a glass display case. "Would you like to buy a necklace to match?" The girl was a well-trained sales person.

"No thanks. Goodbye," Dennis said.

I watched as Angela opened the box that evening and saw her face explode with delight at the sight of my ring. She threw her arms around Dennis's neck and squealed.

"Ohhhh Denny, it's beautiful."

She pulled herself up, wrapped her legs around his hips and kissed him. He moved around in a half circle, smiling and struggling not to fall over from the weight of her body.

"Ooof—my back. You're gonna kill me, Ang. Get down," he said, relief showing on his face when she did.

She stepped back, held out her left hand with the fingers spread apart, and looked at the ring on her finger—my ring.

"Denny, does this mean—?"

"Uh, no, I'm not goin' down on one knee proposing. It's not an engagement ring, just a gift because I love you so much." He raised his palms defensively.

"Well, I just thought—y'know…we've been going together four months now."

"Yeah, time flies, doesn't it?"

"But it's so beautiful, honey. It must have cost a lot. I never imagined having anything like it."

"Hey—I'm not saying it's new, kiddo. Do you mind?"

She pulled my ring from her finger and looked at the inside of the band. "Wow—eighteen carats. What's SR 1962 mean?"

"Not sure. Perhaps the company that made it or a model number. It's a used ring. More classy than modern stuff. Does that bother you Ang?"

"Of course not, darling, but how did you know my size? It's a perfect fit—almost feels like it's holding onto my finger. I feel all tingly and warm."

It is holding you, Angela. Just like it held onto me. It still does.

"Well, I guess it was made just for you, honey," Dennis said.

I was pleased. My ring was given with genuine love this time and what was more important—this young woman would be my new witness. I felt her kindness, sensitivity and empathy. She would understand my message and reveal the truth of what happened to me. I would now have revenge on Gregory, and justice.

I watched as they made passionate love that night and slept in each other's arms. I entered her dream, as I had done to Dennis.

Angela tossed and turned all night, her face distorting with the horror of what I made her see in those nocturnal visions. Her face was pale and drawn the next morning, the whites of her eyes streaked with red.

"I had trouble falling asleep, Den. When I did, I had a terrible dream. It was creepy and so real."

"Yeah, dreams can be weird."

Tell them Angela. Tell them what you saw. Tell them what my husband Gregory Richmond did to me.

She swallowed some pills.

"Den, you didn't forget that I'm spending today with my mother, did you? My parent's anniversary is coming up and she wants to buy a new dress. I'm dying to show my ring to her. I'll call you when I get home."

"Oh yeah. It's Saturday. I forgot. Call me tonight or tomorrow morning. Maybe we can do something." Dennis kissed Angela goodbye. "Your lips are cold," he said.

That night I entered her dreams, again, revealing the vivid images of how I was murdered. She woke up shaking and unwell.

Tell them Angela. Tell them what he did to me. Why won't you tell them?

She didn't call Dennis that day, on Sunday or Monday. On Monday evening her telephone rang.

"Hi Den," she said with a weak, hesitant, trembling voice. "I'm not good. Haven't been well since you left on Saturday morning…Had a terrible migraine and couldn't go out with my mother or to work today…Yes, I told her about the beautiful ring you gave me…I've had dreadful nightmares—horrible things like you can't imagine; then another migraine headache. Couldn't get out of bed or stand the light. Threw up all day. Still feel weak…Had them every night since you left…I dreamt about a woman being murdered in some dark cellar—horribly beaten to death and robbed. I saw the killer's face—a tall, thin, dark-haired, evil-looking man…He stole her purse and jewellery, put the stuff in a bag and walked away. So much blood. She came to me with her head and face hideously mutilated

begging me to help her…Oh darling it was awful…"
"I'm coming right over," he said.

Dennis hugged her when he came in.
"Oh honey. You're shaking," he said.
She burst out in tears. "The same ghastly nightmare repeats every time I go to sleep."
"That's bizarre. I had a similar dream last week."

Why won't you believe, Dennis? Why won't you tell them?

"It feels like a woman's speaking to me from the grave."

Yes, Angela. Listen to my voice. You saw what he did to me. Help me. Tell them what you saw. You must tell them.

"I'll call in sick and stay with you," Dennis said.
I came to her the next two evenings and when she slept in the afternoons, delivering the same visions in her dreams.

Angela. Listen to me. You must tell them. You are my witness.

Angela's eyes were wide and glazed when she woke up screaming like a terrified animal. Worry was etched on Dennis's face.

Angela. Why won't you tell them?

"Honey, I have to go back to work," Dennis said. "Afternoon shift this week. I'll call you tomorrow morning. Make an appointment with your doctor. Maybe he can prescribe something to help you."

I came to her again that night, over and over again.

Angela you must tell them. Why won't you understand?

The next morning she let the phone ring several times before answering it.
"Not good, Den…I see her everywhere. I want her to go away…I have to make her go away…Goodbye. I love you," she said, then

hung up.

The phone rang and rang again. She stared at it but didn't pick up the receiver.

Angela took pen and paper from a drawer in the kitchen, poured a glass of water, picked up a bottle of painkillers, and sat down at her small kitchen table. She swallowed a handful of the tablets, wrote a note in shaky script and folded it. She printed Dennis' name on the paper, removed the ring from her finger, laid it on top of the note and gazed out the window for several minutes.

Dark clouds billowed on the horizon. Horns honked and tires squealed on the street below.

She stood up, ripped one end of the telephone extension cord from the jack on the wall, disconnected the other end from the phone, went into the bedroom and closed the door. I watched her kneel down, tie one end of the cord to the door handle and the other around her neck.

No Angela. Don't.

She pushed her hands into the pockets of her jeans, turned to face away from the door and thrust her body forward. Her face remained a few inches above the carpet in spite of the slight stretching of the cord. She uttered no sound. Her face, with eyes closed, bore a determined look and she made no attempt to withdraw her hands and reverse the action. I watched as the ligature tightened around her neck and she lost consciousness from oxygen deprivation as the cord constricted the arteries in her neck. After ten minutes, her jaw slackened as life slipped away from her body, like mist rising from a lake in the cool morning air.

Why Angela? You were my witness. I wanted you to tell them. We were one—you, my ring and I. Why didn't you tell them?

Fifteen minutes later, the door to the apartment opened. I heard Dennis' frantic voice calling out.

"Angela? Where are you? Angela?"

A light breeze lifted the lace curtains in waves. The hum of traffic drifted up from the street. He stuck his head out the window and looked at the pavement below.

Dennis sat at the kitchen table and glanced at the half-filled glass of water and bottle of pain killers. He picked up the folded piece of paper and my ring. Was she giving it back? Why? He opened the note and read.

Den:
I can't bear it anymore. Have to make the pain go away. I'm sorry darling. Forgive me. I love you. Goodbye.
Ang

He looked at the ring and put it in his pocket.

I saw the look on his face as a terrible foreboding filled him, like ice spreading over the surface of a pond. He picked up the empty pill bottle and looked all around, glancing at wilted potted plants on the credenza and at the food-smeared dishes filling the kitchen sink. He saw the disconnected telephone lying on its side in the corner, its grey extension cord missing; the broken telephone jack hanging from the wall.

"Oh God—no!" he screamed and rushed to the bedroom.

The door was closed. He turned the knob and pushed with all his strength to increase the opening far enough to enter.

The blood must have frozen in his veins when he saw her.

Angela's body lay on the floor; the telephone cord recessed into the flesh of her neck. Purple spots dotted her pallid cheeks and one of her pink fuzzy bedroom slippers lay askew on the carpet where it had slipped off her foot.

Dennis loosened the cord from around her neck and checked her pulse. It was too late.

Sobs racked him and his face twisted with anguish. He cradled her lifeless, still-warm body in his arms and wailed. Her round, beautiful face appeared peaceful. His body rocked back and forth as he caressed her soft, smooth cheeks and combed through her auburn hair with his fingers.

"No! Dear God, No! No! No! Why, Angela? Why?" he screamed.

Yes, Angela—why? I thought that you of all people would understand and tell them what my husband did to me.

The next two days I watched Dennis wade through a swamp of

grief and torment. He endured a long police interview.

"Was the door to Miss Grant's apartment locked when you arrived, Mr. Boyd?"

"Yes.

"How did you get in?"

"I had a key which she gave me."

"Did you and Miss Grant have an argument?"

"No. We loved each other. I was going to ask her to marry me."

"Was she depressed or in debt?"

"No. She had a good job, saved her money and was always positive and cheerful. She wasn't prone to moods."

"Did she use drugs?"

"No. We never touched that stuff."

"What about her family?"

"She was close to her parents and they had a loving relationship."

"Was she worried about anything?"

"No."

"Do you have any idea why she would take her own life, Mr. Boyd?"

"No. None at all."

"There was nothing that upset her recently?"

Now you can tell the authorities Dennis. You and Angela are both witnesses. Explain what happened to me on parking level three of the building on Market Street. Tell them. Tell them, now.

"She was having nightmares that disturbed her, but don't we all at one time or another?"

"Stay available Mr. Boyd. We may have more questions for you."

*

At the funeral, Angela's distraught parents questioned why their daughter would kill herself.

"Angela had everything to live for. She told us how much she loved you Dennis," her mother said, through tears. "We hoped you might have a life together."

Dennis lowered his head. "I loved her. We were happy. Every hour I ask myself the same question. Why?"

Her father touched the closed casket, his agonized face reflecting in the polished wood. "Our world is shattered. She was our only child. There's nothing left for us now," he said, removing his glasses and wiping the tears dripping from his chin.

Angela's framed graduation picture and college diploma rested on a small table next to the casket. I could see the resemblance to her mother—the same wide-set, clear, green eyes, round face and light brown hair. Dennis and Angela's parents held hands, hugged each other and wept at the graveside.

The minister looked at his bible and read a verse from Ecclesiastes. "He has made everything beautiful in its time. He has also set eternity in the human heart; yet no one can fathom what God has done from beginning to end. All we can do is trust in His plan and purpose."

After a pause the minister closed the bible and concluded, "Jesus called Angela home for a reason. In our sorrow we must trust in His goodness, mercy and ultimate design. Blessed be the name of the Lord."

Sobs broke out from the gathering and hands rose to grief-splashed faces. With an empty, crushed look, Dennis stared at the casket.

I'm sorry Dennis. You gave her my ring and made her a witness to my fate. She was a creature too sensitive, good and vulnerable to withstand the sight of such horror. My suffering infused her and she didn't understand that her mission was to secure vengeance and justice for me. I tried with all my power to make her comprehend, but by picking up my ring you assumed the responsibility for passing it to another person.

I know he cannot hear me. No living thing can hear my silent words. The vivid images of my experience can only be conveyed to the possessor of my ring in their dreams.

After Angela's funeral, I came to Dennis each night more vivid, tangible, and insistent each time; a constant somnambulant, suffering companion. I made him see my face pleading for help. He saw Gregory's narrow, ferret-like face with bared teeth and vicious eyes wielding his weapon to crush me. I wrote my initials in blood.

That last night he jerked awake, my vestigial images in his brain. He glanced at the ring on the night table. Its central stone glittered in the moonlight like an all-seeing eye set in a dark socket. He picked it up and looked inside at the band.

"SR. Just like I dreamed."

I saw the look of disbelief on his face as thoughts swirled, then congealed in his mind. He shivered, rubbed his, arms and picked up Angela's picture from the night table. The pieces were coming together now. He was thinking how impossible the idea was, yet couldn't dispel his instinct. His nightmares started when he found the ring. Angela's began when he gave it to her. Now the ring was in his possession again, and the dreams were repeating. An incredible co-incidence?

You must feel it in your bones now, Dennis. Remember Angela's description. Both of you witnessed the murder of the same woman in nocturnal visions—my murder. The murderer, whose face you saw, took a ring from my body—the ring you are now holding—the one you gave to Angela. You know it's true. We are speaking to you, my ring and I; asking for help—for vengeance and justice. The distress was unbearable for Angela and she couldn't speak of what she saw, but you are strong. Tell the authorities what you know, Dennis. Tell them so I can rest. Tell them now.

The vivid memories of those dreams intruded into his waking hours like a macabre slide show. The mental images distracted him. He staggered through his days in a fog, unfit to work or drive.

Why are you resisting the truth Dennis? Tell them. Tell them what you see each night and remember in your waking hours.

It was after a close call while driving that Dennis decided to do it—tell them what he knew. I wonder if he sensed that finding and punishing my murderer would bring peace to us both. Did he think of Angela and feel responsible? It was his fault after all. He must have regretted finding the ring and giving it to her. By doing so she became my ally and witness. My ring was beautiful, but to him it was just a thing, after all, like all the other items he had found in the street. He didn't know how special a ring it was.

Tell them Dennis. Then we can both rest.

The next morning, I saw the exhaustion from restless sleep and turmoil on his face as he wrestled with internal conflict—doubt battling compelling instinct. He still had reservations. Had a woman been murdered or had he imagined it all? Was he insane? Was Angela deranged? He slipped my ring on the little finger of his left hand.

Now we are one, Dennis. You and I. Can you feel the force creeping into each sinew and tendon of your body? The sense that my murder really did happen and that you and Angela witnessed it is too real to dismiss, isn't it? That's why you are here now, but you are wondering if they will believe you. They will believe you Dennis. They must.

He hesitated on mounting the stairs leading to the front door of the precinct station, turned the ring around on his finger and closed his fist around the gems so that only the gold band was visible.

The cop leaned back in his chair. "I'm Officer Derek Lassiter," he said.

"I'm Dennis Boyd. I called you earlier."

"Yes. Thanks for coming in Mr. Boyd. You indicated on the telephone that you wanted to report a crime?"

Tell them Dennis. Tell them what happened to me.

"I have information about a murder."

The cop straightened and his chair creaked as he came forward.

"Oh? What murder is that?"

"A woman who was brutally killed in this city."

It was me. Sarah Richmond.

"Where?"

"I don't know the location. In a building at level three near an elevator. I think it was an underground parking garage."

It was, Dennis. On Market Street.

Lassiter's eyes widened. "When did this take place?"

"I don't know that either," said Dennis.

It was August 12, 1966, Dennis.

"Who do you think was murdered?"
Dennis placed his right hand over the closed fist of his left.
"I don't know her name, but she was blond, early thirties I'd guess, and her initials might be S.R."

It was me. Sarah Richmond.

The cop's eyebrows lifted and the pleasant look on his face changed to one of focused, professional interest. "How do you know those might be her initials, Mr. Boyd?"
"They're on a ring that I'm certain belonged to her."
"Why do you think that?"
Dennis licked his lips and swallowed. "Uh…I just know it, that's all."

You know, Dennis because you have my ring and saw me in your dreams.

Lassiter rolled a pen in his fingers. "Indeed? Can you describe this ring?"
Dennis fidgeted in his seat, squeezed his hands and cleared his throat. "I have it."
The cop stopped writing and his mouth opened. He extended his hand. "You have it? Let me see it."
Dennis raised his left hand and opened it. Lassiter's eyes widened. He opened a drawer of his desk, removed a file folder and opened it.
"Yes, the description matches one owned by a murdered woman. A large, central stone circled with diamonds and emeralds. Take it off and give it to me."
Dennis pulled at the ring but couldn't remove it from his finger or turn it.

We are bound together now, Dennis.

Lassiter's voice elevated. "Take the ring off, I said."
Beads of perspiration seeped from Dennis's forehead as he tried to remove the ring. "I can't. It's too tight."

"Why did you put it on your finger?"

"I didn't want to lose it."

Lassiter got up, took Dennis's hand, and pulled at the ring with no success.

"How long have you been wearing it?"

"I only put it on an hour ago."

"Impossible. It's so tight it's like you've been wearing it for years. It'll have to be cut off. Any markings on the inside of the band?"

"An eighteen-carat mark is stamped there with the letters SR 1962 engraved beside it."

Lassiter glanced at the file again. "Yes, that also matches the description."

My initials and the date of our marriage.

Lassiter sat down, pulled out a pad of paper and started writing. "Where did you find this ring?"

"On the street."

"Where? What street?"

"Near the corner of Tenth and Market Streets."

Where it fell from Gregory's pocket, Dennis.

"The business district. You should have turned it in when you found it, Mr. Boyd."

Dennis swallowed. "Yeah, I suppose so."

"What's your occupation Mr. Boyd?"

"I have a job with the City Works Department."

"What else do you know about this murder, Mr. Boyd?"

"The killer stole other jewellery from her body, but not her earrings."

That fiend Gregory wouldn't touch the crushed mess of my head to remove them.

Lassiter straightened up. "You know that she was wearing other jewellery?"

"Yes—a necklace and bracelet, I think."

The cop stared at Dennis and nodded. "So the killer robbed her and you know what jewellery he took. I see. Anything else?"

Tell him it was my husband Gregory, Dennis. Tell him.

"The murderer was a skinny, dark haired man, about six feet tall with a pencil thin moustache—cruel looking. He killed her with a metal bar or pipe."

The cop blinked several times, and then his eyes narrowed. "How do you know all this Mr. Boyd?"

Dennis hesitated. "I, uh…saw it in a dream."

Yes Dennis. I made you see it.

Lassiter smiled and dropped his pen on the desk. "You dreamed that you saw this woman murdered and you found her ring lying in the street. Is that what you're saying?"

"Yes, that's right."

Of course. You are my witness, Dennis.

"Do you use drugs, Mr. Boyd?"

Dennis blinked. "Uh, no—never."

Lassiter's eyes narrowed. "Where were you on the evening of Friday, August 12th, Mr. Boyd?"

Dennis squirmed in his chair.

"With my girlfriend."

"You remember exactly where you were on that night?"

"Yeah. She and I spent every Friday evening and most weekends together."

The cop lifted his pen. "What's your girlfriend's name and address?"

"Angela Grant—but—"

"Grant? That name sounds familiar." Lassiter's brow gathered and his chair squeaked as he pressed against the back.

He got up, removed a folder from a file cabinet and opened it.

"A woman by that name was found dead three weeks ago—an apparent suicide. It says here that a man named Dennis Boyd discovered her body. That was you? She was your girlfriend?"

Dennis buried his face in his hands. "Yes. I called the police when

I found her. They interviewed me and I told them everything I knew at the time."

"A young woman taking her own life—tragic. It must have been a terrible experience for you." He stared at Dennis for a few moments and leaned back in his chair.

"Since she's deceased, obviously Angela Grant can't verify you were with her on the evening of August 12th, then."

"Well…no. She can't."

Lassiter rose from his desk, opened the door and motioned to a plain-clothed man sitting at a desk. The two had a brief discussion outside the room. They looked in Dennis's direction. The plain-clothed man nodded and glanced at Dennis as Lassiter spoke to him. Dennis squirmed in his chair.

The two officers came back and closed the door.

"Mr. Boyd this is detective Sinclair," said Lassiter.

Dennis nodded at the man.

"Hello Mr. Boyd," Sinclair said with a flat tone, not smiling. "Let me see the ring."

Dennis opened his hand. Sinclair looked at the ring.

"No wonder you can't remove it. The band's pressed tight into the flesh of your finger."

"I can't explain it. It feels like it's crushing it."

"Do you have high blood pressure or edema that would make your body swell?"

"No to the first thing. What's the second mean?"

Sinclair ignored the question and nodded to Lassiter.

Lassiter grinned. "You've been very helpful to us, Dennis—very helpful indeed."

Dennis relaxed and exhaled. He seemed confident that they believed him. "I'm glad. Do you know who was murdered?"

You know who was murdered, Dennis. Tell them.

"Yes, we do. The woman's family posted a reward for information leading to the arrest of her killer. Did you know that?"

"No, I didn't."

The cops looked at each other. "Are you sure about that, Mr. Boyd? Is there anything else you want to tell us?"

"No. I've told you everything I know."

Sinclair moved close to Dennis and placed a hand on his shoulder. "Mr. Boyd, we are arresting you for the murder of Sarah Richmond."

I saw the spectre of fright invade Dennis's eyes and the colour evaporate from his face.

Tell them it wasn't you Dennis. They've made a mistake. It was Gregory Richmond, my husband.

"No. I didn't kill her. I had nothing to do with it."

"You know things only Sarah's killer would, Mr. Boyd and you have her ring which you claimed to have found."

"I did find it. I found it on the street."

"There was media coverage of Sarah's killing at the time of her death, but we withheld details from the public about how she was killed and what was taken from her, except to say that robbery was the apparent motive. You know what was taken and how she was murdered. You intended to rob her and when she resisted, you killed her and stole her jewellery. Admit it. What did you do with the rest of it?"

Dennis raised his open left hand. It trembled.

"All I have is this ring. Like I said, I found it in the street."

"We received a call from a pawnbroker that a man of your description tried to pawn a ring matching the one stolen from Sarah Richmond."

"I wanted to know if it was valuable, that's all."

"You ran from the store when he went to use the telephone."

"I was worried I would get into trouble for not turning it in when I found it."

"Only guilty people run away. Admit it was you, Dennis. You killed her didn't you?"

Dennis swallowed and his breathing quickened. He shook his head.

"No. I told you I saw it happen in a dream. You must believe me."

Lassiter smiled. "You expect anyone to believe that? You've been reading too many spooky stories."

"I saw the killer's face. I'll recognize it if I see his picture. I think it was someone she knew."

The two officers looked at each other.

"We interviewed Angela Grant's parents after her death," Sinclair said. "They recalled their daughter telling them that her boyfriend had given her an expensive ring which was not in her possession at the time of her death. That person was you and the ring you gave her was the one you stole from Sarah Richmond when you murdered her."

"Yes, I gave her the ring, but I found it. I didn't kill that woman."

"If you found it, and weren't the murderer you could have turned it in."

"I should have, but didn't do the honest thing."

"Miss Grant knew you robbed and killed Sarah Richmond didn't she?"

"No, because I didn't kill that woman."

"You fell out with Angela Grant and she threatened to expose what you did. To keep her quiet, you killed her, made it look like suicide and took back the ring."

Tell them Angela killed herself and why, Dennis.

"No. Angela committed suicide. I think she had the same dreams as I did about that woman being murdered. The images upset her so much she couldn't stand it and killed herself."

"A pretty fantastic story, Mr. Boyd. Have you ever had a psychiatric examination?"

"No. I'm not crazy."

"The fact is that when you heard about the reward money you concocted an unbelievable story about finding the ring and dreaming that both you and your girlfriend witnessed the murder. You murdered two women and were hoping to incriminate an innocent man in Sarah Richmond's murder with a phoney description. You're a sick man, Mr. Boyd."

I saw the distress on Dennis' face. His eyes were large with fear and his breathing quickened. Streaks of perspiration ran down his cheeks and his hands clenched together, whitening the knuckles.

"No—I—I—ah—ah..." He stuttered and his eyes blinked rapidly. He gasped and stopped speaking.

"Mr. Boyd?" Sinclair said.

Dennis tried to speak. "I-I-I-ah-ah-ah-wh-wha—?"

"Mr. Boyd? Are you all right?" Lassiter said.

Dennis's head slumped to one side. His mouth twisted open and a silver strand of drool dripped from one corner onto his shirt. His left eyelid sagged. He started to shake; his eyes rolled back into his head as he went into seizure.

"Call an ambulance," Detective Sinclair said.

Dennis slid to the floor. His head made a dull thud as it struck the seat of the wooden chair. A large, wet spot expanded on the front of his trousers.

They transported him to the hospital and posted a police guard outside his room.

I hovered above the bed until he died, watching the life leave his body like smoke rising from the dying embers of a fire.

I'm sorry Dennis. I'm sorry for Angela too. You were my witnesses. My ring and I made you see what happened to me and I believed you would tell others and avenge me.

It must have been cold in the compartment where they stored Dennis' body, but I could not feel it as I hovered above his white-sheet draped corpse with the tag attached to the big toe. The next day I watched doctors autopsy his body, cut open the chest, and remove the organs. They used a saw to remove the top of his skull and extract the brain.

"He died from a ruptured brain aneurysm resulting in a massive cerebral hemorrhage," one said.

They cut my ring from his finger and I followed as it was delivered to the police station.

Lassiter and Sinclair sat reviewing the case file. My ring, in a small plastic bag sat on the table in front of them.

Sinclair picked it up. "Beautiful piece. Very unusual. Gives me an odd feeling to touch it."

"Yeah, me too. I keep thinking about the morning we discovered that woman. Worst murder scene I ever saw."

"Pretty messy. But there's no doubt we've found our man," said

Sinclair.

"That Boyd character was as guilty as hell. Too bad he didn't dance at the end of a rope for murdering those two women."

You're both wrong, but it doesn't matter now. When my ring passes to other hands I will have a new witness.

"Why would someone concoct such a ridiculous story in an effort to claim the reward money? Did he really think anyone would believe that?" Sinclair said.

"Criminals are stupid and some are mentally ill, that's why. That guy was either Grade A stupid or bonkers."

"I think we can close the Richmond file. The Grant dossier will have to remain classified as a suicide."

"I think Boyd strangled her and then strung her up on the doorknob to make it look like suicide."

"I agree, but there's not enough hard evidence to substantiate murder."

"Let's wrap it. You've informed Sarah Richmond's parents?"

"Yeah. They've cancelled the fifty-thousand dollar reward they posted for information leading to the arrest of the person who killed their daughter."

"How'd they take the news?"

"Pleased that the killer was found, but still hurting. Nothing will bring their child back and her murder was so horrific and senseless."

"At least they won't have to sit through a trial."

"Yeah, but dying like he did was too good for Boyd."

"Sarah Richmond's husband been informed?"

"Yes."

Gregory's plan worked. An innocent person dead for the murder he committed. My murder.

"Was he ever a suspect?"

"Interviewed as routine procedure, but no evidence pointed to him and there was no indication of marital discord. Sarah Richmond was well-off and had a large insurance policy but arranged it of her own volition. The husband seemed pretty broken up when advised of his wife's death."

A put-on theatrical act of grief. Gregory has everything now—my house and all my assets. I loved him, thought he loved me in return, and left him everything I owned in my will. When we married, the minister said it was till death do us part, but I didn't imagine it was my foul murder by his design that would separate us so soon. I wonder who he's with now? Does she know the evil creature she shares a bed and her body with?

I watched as Gregory entered the room in the police station two days later. He's gained weight. I can see it in his face. One of his wrists bears an expensive watch; the other, a thick gold bracelet as he extends his hand to the officers. He displays the quick, furtive movements of a weasel hunting prey. His cunning eyes glow in their sockets like obsidian in the moonlight and a slight smile betrays his voracity. My boiling hatred for him mixes with delirious excitement at his presence. It can mean only one thing.

"Good morning officers. I've come to claim my wife's ring that you've recovered."

Yes. Take the ring, Gregory. Hold the thing you pulled from my body the night you murdered me; the object which is an inseparable part of my existence. I've waited so long for this moment.

ABOUT THE AUTHOR

Raymond Holmes was born and raised in Toronto and lives in Brampton, Ontario. Following careers in technology, he started writing on retirement, in spite of being seriously challenged by English grammar. Heeding the traditional sage advice of 'write what you know,' Raymond started penning memoir pieces until he realized that detailing the events of his pedestrian life might draw limited interest from the literary community.

A foray into playwriting met with some success. His plays *Boris and Herman*, *The Pooman* and *The Lonely Vigil of Emily Baxter* were performed at the South Simcoe Theatre in Cookstown, Ontario each earning a modest honorarium. The last play listed above went on to even greater success, winning third prize plus a reading in the 2013 Ottawa Little Theatre playwriting contest.

Hopes of financial security and rubbing shoulders with playwrights such as Neil Simon on Broadway were later dashed as no other of his masterworks for the stage were taken up by other theatres. Raymond now entered his short story writing phase assisted by a reference book on English grammar. Pieces were published in *The Northern Appeal*, a bi-annual Simcoe County literary journal, and *Unleashed Ink II*, an anthology of short stories and poetry published by the Barrie Writers Club.

This is Raymond's first book of short stories and he continues to write others. A collection of novellas is in the works, but to date he has made no attempt to approach the seven-story mountain of novel writing.

He has been happily married to Mary for over thirty years and has maintained a lifetime love of cats, classical music and chocolate, not necessarily in that order.

LOOK FOR UPCOMING WORKS FROM RAY HOLMES
THROUGH MIDDLEROAD PUBLISHERS

MORE BOOKS FROM MIDDLEROAD PUBLISHERS

"Making literature see the light of day."

RACING WITH THE RAIN

available on Amazon

"Ken Puddicombe's brilliant novel Racing with the Rain evokes not only personal consequences of an historic political conflict in Guyana, during the Cold War, but also the cold cynicism and tragic irony of a small, defenseless Caribbean state being sacrificed to super-power hegemony." -Frank Birbalsingh, author of Novels and The Nation: Essays in Canadian Literature.

JUNTA

available on Amazon

"After a first novel—"Racing in the Rain" (2012)— introducing a Caribbean, steaming in post-colonial turbulence, Ken Puddicombe follows up with Junta, another suspenseful tale of churning political chaos..." –Frank Birbalsingh author of Novels and The Nation: Essays in Canadian Literature.

DOWN INDEPENDENCE BOULEVARD AND OTHER STORIES

available on Amazon

"Ken Puddicombe's brilliant collection of stories tells the tales of people forced to leave their homes and while enjoying freedom in a faraway country, they crave the past, the known and predictable...it is the universality of their destiny that comes across, escaping from racial conflicts or dictatorship of any kind from anywhere in the world." —Judith Kopácsi Gelberger, author of *Heroes Don't Cry.*

PERFECT EXECUTION AND OTHER STORIES

available on Amazon

Brampton Author Michael Joll has written an appealing and diverse first collection of short stories that span several continents and encompasses the gamut of human emotions.

PEOPLE OF GUYANA

available on Amazon

Guyanese poets Ian McDonald and Peter Jailall have turned out moving poems about a diverse mix of Guyana's colourful characters, folk lore, and history. From Berbice to Essequibo, and Demerara in-between, these poems traverse the geography of Guyana with startling insights into its people and culture.